"You can't keep escaping me, Brenna."

She couldn't get his arms from about her. They were like steel bands against her pulling fingers, until suddenly Nathan thrust her away from him. "I don't understand you. I doubt I ever will." His hands clenched into fists at his sides. "I loved you.... And when a man offers his love and his life it's usually polite at least to tell him you don't want them!"

But Brenna had been afraid to face Nathan with her refusal to marry him. And she was still afraid. If Nathan was able to persuade her into bed again, she wouldn't be able to deny him anything.

She turned accusing eyes on him. "I'm here because my sister's marriage is in trouble," she grated. "But once that's settled again, I'm leaving."

CAROLE MORTIMER, one of our most popular—and prolific—English authors, began writing for the Harlequin Presents series in 1979. She now has more than forty top-selling romances to her credit and shows no signs whatsoever of running out of plot ideas. She writes strong traditional romances with a distinctly modern appeal, and her winning way with characters and romantic plot twists has earned her an enthusiastic following worldwide.

Books by Carole Mortimer

HARLEQUIN PRESENTS

757—UNTAMED
773—AN UNWILLING DESIRE
780—A PAST REVENGE
786—THE PASSIONATE LOVER
797—TEMPESTUOUS AFFAIR
804—CHERISH TOMORROW
812—A NO RISK AFFAIR
829—LOVERS IN THE AFTERNOON
852—THE DEVIL'S PRICE
860—LADY SURRENDER
877—KNIGHT'S POSSESSION
892—DARKNESS INTO LIGHT
909—NO LONGER A DREAM

HARLEQUIN SIGNATURE EDITION

GYPSY

These books may be available at your local bookseller.

Don't miss any of our special offers. Write to us at the following address for information on our newest releases.

Harlequin Reader Service
901 Fuhrmann Blvd., P.O. Box 1397, Buffalo, NY 14240
Canadian address: P.O. Box 603,
Fort Erie, Ont. L2A 9Z9

CAROLE MORTIMER

the wade dynasty

Harlequin Books

TORONTO • NEW YORK • LONDON
AMSTERDAM • PARIS • SYDNEY • HAMBURG
STOCKHOLM • ATHENS • TOKYO • MILAN

For John,
Matthew and Joshua

Harlequin Presents first edition October 1986
ISBN 0-373-10923-7

Original hardcover edition published in 1986
by Mills & Boon Limited

CHAPTER ONE

'IF I assure you I no longer imagine myself in love with you will you stop running away and come home where you belong?'

Brenna froze on the rock where she sat, even the seagulls overhead seeming to stop their cries, as if they sensed the sudden tension of the young woman who, until a few seconds ago, had been sketching the beauty of their flight over the tranquillity of the grey-green of the Irish sea in midsummer.

Nathan. She knew that voice in a dozen or more different emotions, the rich timbre of his Canadian accent now faintly mocking. She had known him as the brother, the adversary, the arrogant tormentor, and finally the lover. And she knew from the tone of his voice now that the second most suited his mood at the moment.

Why had he come for her now, why had he left it over a year since she had walked—no, *run* away from him? Because she had run that Easter sixteen months ago, had scurried back to England as if the very devil were at her heels. The first time she had looked at Nathan Wade she had thought him in league with the devil, his faded denims snug on his leanly muscled hips, the black, dusty shirt taut across the power of his chest, piercing grey eyes delving into her soul as he looked at her beneath the black, dusty and sweat-stained stetson that was tilted low across his forehead.

Until that moment Brenna had only seen cowboys on television or in films, with the good guys wearing the white hats and the bad guys wearing the black ones; she hadn't needed Nathan's black hat to tell her he was a bad guy, had known just from looking at him that if it had been the last century Nathan Wade would have been a cold-hearted gun-slinger on the wrong side of the law. Instead he now masqueraded as a Canadian rancher, his ancestors having moved from the wide open spaces of America to its even wider and less crowded neighbour, two generations ago. They now owned land and wielded considerable power in their adopted county!

And Nathan had sought to own her, to help forge the dynasty that his brother and her sister were even now in the process of continuing, and their first baby was due in two months' time.

It was strange the surprises Fate held in store for the unsuspecting. Until she was twelve years of age Brenna had lived quite happily in England with her older sister and their divorced mother, barely noticing the absence of the irresponsible man who was her father, the father who accepted no ties in his life, not even that of remaining faithful for more than a couple of months at a time to his wife and the two daughters she had borne him. Their divorce had barely registered with either eleven-year-old Brenna or thirteen-year-old Lesli; they had not seen any less of their father then because he had rarely been at home anyway. But the advent of Patrick Wade into all their lives almost a year later hadn't been as smooth. The rich Canadian rancher had demanded that Anna and her two daughters go back to Canada with him to the ranch he owned several miles from Calgary.

For the first time that anyone could remember, Andrew Jordan made a conscious decision; he didn't want his two daughters moving anywhere!

If he had known Patrick Wade a little better he would have realised that the harshly handsome man had never been denied anything in his life, that what he wanted he always got, one way or another. He had got Anna and her two daughters.

And Brenna and Lesli had acquired two of the most arrogantly self-assured stepbrothers that could ever have been wished on anyone. As they were already grown men of twenty-six and twenty-three, respectively, perhaps it was to be expected that Nathan and Grant had little patience for the two young English girls who had become part of their family.

How Brenna wished it had always remained that way!

But Grant and Leslie had suddenly fallen in love four years ago, and in the face of Brenna's distrust of all the Wade men it had seemed like a betrayal. And when Nathan had come after her sixteen months ago, she had run as far and as fast as she could go. It looked as if her running was over, at least as far as Nathan was concerned. If she could believe what Nathan was saying, he had changed his mind about marrying her. She had always known he wasn't motivated by love.

She took one last wistful look at the calmness of the water off the north-west coast of England, knowing Nathan still stood behind and above her. Brenna had climbed down the cliff to sit on a jutting rock as she did her sketching, enjoying the wildness of this rugged beauty, alone in this secluded cove, but not feeling in the least lonely. She loved everything about England, and even after six years in Canada had felt immediately at home as soon as she stepped off the plane in London on her way to college four years ago. She had no intention of returning to Canada, it wasn't where she 'belonged'.

She drew up her knees with her sketch-pad on, regretting that she wasn't going to be able to finish her drawing, unzipping the leather pouch that lay on the flatness of the rock beside her and putting her equipment carefully inside. Just because she was going to have to turn and face Nathan again after sixteen months, there was no reason not to take her usual care with putting away her work!

'Brenna!'

The harsh command of his voice wasn't lazily mocking this time, the impatience that was never far from the surface of his decisive nature ripping coldly into her.

She knew she had no choice now but to turn and face him, that if she didn't, he was going to come down here after her. She prepared herself for the confrontation as best she could, getting slowly to her feet, small and slender in the tight denims and green T-shirt, her hair a wild tumble of ebony down her spine, eyes the colour of darkest emeralds seeking him out. No amount of preparation could have prepared her for the lean figure that stood on top of the cliff, the midday sun behind him making him appear only as a dark silhouette. It was enough.

Brenna drew in a shuddering breath, blinking coal-black lashes that fanned out thickly from the almond shape of her eyes as they fleetingly touched her cheek. She could see Nathan a little better now her eyes had become accustomed to the bright sunshine. He stood in the shadow, but she knew his harshly handsome beauty as if by heart, hair as black as her own, black brows jutting out over icy grey eyes, a long straight nose, high cheekbones that looked as if they could have belonged to some unclaimed Indian ancestry, a sculptured mouth that rarely laughed, his smiles cynical at best, and a square chin that laid claim to his arrogance. He was wearing a black, Western-style suit, although the jacket was dangling over his shoulder held by a single finger in the heat of this August day, the black and white checked shirt stretching tautly across his chest as he did so, the black boots slightly dusty from his walk from the road to the cove. Brenna knew that at a couple of inches over six feet, he stood a foot taller than her, but at the moment it looked like three times that!

While she had been studying him he had taken the same time to look at her, his eyes narrowed as he met her challenging gaze.

Had he noticed any changes in her since their parting at the airport all those months ago? She could see none in him, he looked as harshly forbidding as usual. She knew there had been few changes in her either, except perhaps that her hair was even longer than before, impractically reaching almost to her waist. And unfashionably too, when all her friends were going for a variety of much shorter styles. But it was a vanity that she was loath to part with, a gentle breeze from the sea behind her stirring the slightly wavy tresses about the small oval of her face.

'I'm not running away,' she told him firmly, almost defiantly, she realised angrily. But Nathan had always had the power to put her on the defensive, and she realised their months apart hadn't changed that. 'And I'm perfectly happy where I am,' she added with dismissal for his claim of her home being in Canada.

Nathan chose to read her claim literally, dark brows rising as he looked pointedly at her precarious position on the rock. 'I think perhaps you might be a little more comfortable up here,' he drawled, reaching out a hand to help her up beside him.

Brenna looked at that hand as if it were a snake about to strike, not wanting any sort of physical contact with him. So instead of taking his hand, she slapped her leather pouch into it before scrambling up the cliff beside him, dusting the dirt from her hands as she realised her flat trainers put her on a level with his shoulder. Great, now she felt like a twelve-year-old again!

She kept her distance from him, her head tilted back to look at him. 'How did you find me?' she asked.

'I went to the cottage where you're staying, your friend told me,' he watched her with pebble-hard eyes.

Brenna stiffened at the way he said 'friend'. 'What's wrong, Nathan? Aren't my friends good enough for you?' she said scornfully.

'*Is* he good?' he bit out harshly.

'He?' she frowned.

'Your lover,' he said contemptuously.

Her frown darkened ominously. 'Just who did you talk to at the house?' she snapped.

Nathan shrugged dismissively. 'I believe he said his name was Nick.'

Brenna shot him a resentful glance, hating him more than ever for his assumption. '*Carolyn* happens to be my friend,' she bit out precisely. 'Nick Bancroft is her fiancé.'

'That's very liberal of her,' he rasped.

'You——'

'Let's not get into an argument here,' he told her patronisingly. 'I would hate one—or both—of us, to go over the side of this cliff.'

It didn't surprise her that he had known that was just what she would like to do to him. 'Then don't make assumptions,' she ground out angrily.

'I'll try not to,' he drawled. 'But when a young man answers the door of the cottage I've been told you're a guest at, what else was I supposed to think?'

Ever since she had reached sixteen years of age

she had had to contend with Nathan's over-protectiveness where boys were concerned, when, after years of taking no notice of her, he had suddenly decided to offer her a big brother's protection, a protection she hadn't wanted then and deeply resented now. Even if Nick had been her lover instead of Carolyn's it was none of this man's business—she was twenty-two, not sixteen! Besides, it was protection from him she had needed—and not received.

'Maybe you should have asked.' Her eyes flashed her resentment.

Grey eyes warred with green for several seconds, until finally Nathan sighed heavily, running an impatient hand through the overlong hair he was somehow always forgetting to have cut. But the longer style suited the harshness of his face, slightly softening those intimidating features, the lines that indicated that he had lived a hard thirty-six years for all his wealth. 'I didn't come here to discuss your lovers—or lack of them,' he added at her rebellious expression.

Somehow even that sounded like an insult. 'Then why are you here?' she asked impatiently, taking her leather pouch from him to begin walking up the hill to the cottage Carolyn had rented for the month.

'Lesli has walked out on Grant and I have reason to think she's coming to you.'

If Nathan, a man who lashed with his tongue rather than his hands, had struck her hard across the face she couldn't have been more stunned, coming to an abrupt halt before she whipped around to face him. He hadn't moved, silhouetted against the grey-green sea now. 'Lesli has left Grant?' she repeated disbelievingly; Lesli had always worshipped the ground Grant walked over.

Nathan gave an abrupt inclination of his head. 'Three days ago. You obviously knew nothing about it,' he sighed at the realisation.

Lesli had left Grant? It was unthinkable. Her sister adored the man, had given up the idea of law school as soon as he had asked her to marry him, and had never seemed to regret that decision, becoming the perfect rancher's wife only three months before their parents were killed in a light aeroplane crash only five miles from the ranch. She had continued that way for the last four years.

'I don't believe it,' Brenna shook her head. 'Lesli would never leave Grant.'

'Believe me, she has,' Nathan drawled.

'But *why*?' she groaned.

He shrugged. 'They had an argument—and don't ask me what about, Grant told me to stay out of it when I asked him,' he revealed drily.

Brenna could believe that; Grant was as arrogant as his brother. 'You said you believe she was coming here?' she prompted faintly.

'She was booked on the flight that should have landed two days ago.'

'Then she's in London,' Brenna groaned.

'All I know is that she was booked on the flight, the airline wouldn't tell me whether or not she actually got on it,' he explained grimly.

'Wouldn't or couldn't?' she scorned.

'Wouldn't,' he repeated softly, dangerously. 'The dictates of security. Do you really think now is the time for an argument about what the Wade money can or cannot buy?'

Colour darkened her cheeks as he correctly guessed the reason for her derision. She had learnt early in life what power the Wade name and money wielded, and even ten years later she hadn't been able to bury her bitterness. In fact, it had increased.

She swallowed hard. 'If Grant wanted you to stay out of it why didn't he come after her himself?' she demanded resentfully.

'I told you, we aren't sure she actually got on that flight, and if she didn't then whoever came here was going to have a wasted journey. If she changed her mind and went home Grant wanted to be there.'

'Waiting for her,' she rasped.

Anger flared in the silver-grey eyes. 'You make it sound as if he intends beating her as soon as he gets his hands on her,' Nathan snapped harshly.

'For daring to leave him?' Brenna questioned tautly. 'It's a possibility.'

Nathan's mouth tightened. 'Don't be so damned stupid!' he said caustically. 'I don't believe anything can be solved by running away,' his tone was accusing. 'But even I would hesitate to hit a woman seven months pregnant with my child!'

The cutting rejoinder she had been about to make in retaliation to his 'running away' remark fled her mind at the mention of Lesli's pregnancy. 'Heavens, I'd forgotten for a moment,' she moaned. 'Where could she have gone?' Worry darkened her eyes.

'Well, it's obvious that if she did come in on that plane she wasn't able to persuade your landlady to tell her where you were.'

'As you were,' she put in drily.

'Brenna——'

'I'm sorry,' she grimaced. 'Force of habit.'

'I'm aware of that,' he rasped.

'I said I was sorry,' she glared.

'And that makes everything all right?' Nathan demanded tersely.

Brenna was aware that he had seen a double meaning to her apology—and taken it. 'You said you were over that,' she avoided the piercing ice of his eyes, knowing how he must have hated being thwarted a year ago when she hadn't returned to Canada as she was expected to.

'That?' he gave a harsh snort. 'What's the matter, Brenna, can't you even use the word love?'

Her chin rose challengingly. 'Not in connection with you, no!'

A dangerous glitter narrowed his eyes. 'Then it's as well I am "over that", isn't it?' he bit out harshly. 'Otherwise you just might have hurt my feelings, mightn't you?'

The idea of anyone or anything being able to pierce this man's heart and actually find any softer emotions that *could* be hurt was as laughable as his derisive tone implied.

'Did you try the hotels in town?' Brenna returned to the subject of Lesli, not willing to get into an argument with Nathan about what had happened sixteen months ago, and the fact that she hadn't returned to Calgary when college finished that summer as she had told Nathan she would.

'All the major ones,' he nodded. 'None of them had a Mrs Wade or a Miss Jordan registered, which means that if she is in London she has no intention of being found until she's good and ready. Which leaves you,' he reasoned. 'Wherever she is, here or still in Canada, she'll be in touch with you some time in the near future; the Jordan sisters always stick together,' he added derisively.

She knew he was referring to the fact that although she hadn't been back to Canada the last year, she had telephoned her sister regularly once a month just to let her know she was all right, had even written a couple of times. She had made no such contact with Nathan, and Lesli had promised not to give him her address. Her eyes widened as she realised that.

'Grant and I searched out a few of those letters from you that Lesli has been hoarding the last year,' Nathan drawled as he guessed the reason for her accusing look.

'You read my letters to Lesli?' she gasped, desperately trying to remember all that she had said in them; little about Nathan, she was sure.

His expression darkened. 'No,' he rasped. 'Although I had the right; when you left you promised to marry me!'

'I said I would be back in the summer and we could talk about it!' she corrected heatedly. 'Obviously I decided we didn't even need to talk about it!'

'Wouldn't it have been more polite to come back and tell me that yourself?' he ground out.

She hadn't felt able to do that, had feared—yes, *feared* that he might be able to persuade her into bed as he had during her Easter break at home. Because she knew if he managed to share her bed again she wouldn't be able to deny him anything. Even now she could vividly remember the strength of his lean body wrapped about hers, the musky male scent of him as his mouth nuzzled against her neck. The memories of that night hadn't faded at all during the last sixteen months away from him.

'We had nothing to talk about,' she dismissed in a hard voice.

'I'd told you that I loved you!' he reminded her tautly.

And that claim had caused her more pain than happiness; it still did! 'And as you can now say you don't, it's as well I didn't take you seriously,' she derided. 'Now could we, for once, stop bringing our conversation back to a personal level and concentrate on Lesli and the fact that she's alone somewhere and seven months pregnant?'

Nathan gave an abrupt inclination of his head. 'I'll have to call Grant and let him know I've had no luck finding her here.'

And Brenna could see how much admitting that failure irked him. 'You can do that once we get back to London,' she snapped. 'Right now Lesli is the important one.'

His mouth thinned. 'Grant is suffering too, you know,' he rasped.

'Of course,' she scorned. 'After all, Lesli is carrying the Wade heir! It wasn't enough to make him leave his prize herd, was it?' she accused.

'Brenna——'

'Oh, let's get back to the cottage so that I can get my things together,' she bit out impatiently. 'I'd like to get back to London this afternoon.'

He grabbed her arm and swung her round to face him, his features contorted with anger. 'If Lesli leaving Grant had anything to do with you I promise you you'll regret it!' he threatened harshly.

Brenna frowned. 'What do you mean?'

'You've shown your contempt of the Wade family for so long maybe a little of it rubbed off on Lesli. Maybe I *should* have read those letters!'

Her eyes shot flames at him. 'If Lesli has come to her senses and no longer sees you and Grant as big fearless heroes, then all I can say is it's about time!' she challenged. 'But I can assure you nothing I've said influenced her; I've been telling her for years that you're both arrogant sons-of——'

'Your success as an illustrator of children's books doesn't seem to have moderated your language any,' Nathan bit out grimly. 'Your mouth still needs washing out with soap!'

Brenna's eyes flashed like emeralds. 'And who taught me every curse in the book?'

His mouth thinned. 'I always told Dad he should have kept you away from the ranch hands.'

'I was referring to their boss!'

He gave a deep sigh. 'A lot of things can go wrong on a ranch,' he defended.

'And you swear about every one,' she recalled softly, her expression hardening as she realised she sounded almost wistful. 'How did you know about my illustrating?' she bit out.

He shrugged. 'Lesli was very proud of her baby sister's accomplishments,' he drawled. 'The copy of the book that you sent her has been put by for the baby.'

'What did you think about it?' she mumbled.

Grey eyes glinted with humour. '*Koly the Koala* is not exactly my taste in literature.'

'No,' she snapped. 'I remember Mum throwing out of the house a few of your ideas of literature,' she scorned.

'They were Grant's,' he rasped. 'He brought them back from university.'

'And you didn't even glance at them,' taunted Brenna.

'Oh, I glanced at them,' Nathan drawled derisively. 'But they were giving me an inferiority complex; I didn't realise most of those positions were possible!'

Carolyn had got back from the village during their absence, and Brenna made the introductions Nathan had been in too much of a hurry to bother with when he arrived. Carolyn, beautiful blonde, blue-eyed Carolyn, had difficulty hiding her surprise at the sudden appearance of a stepbrother she had never heard of.

'Although I don't blame you for keeping him a secret, darling,' her friend told her as she put her arm in the crook of Nathan's, smiling up at him warmly. 'He's beautiful!' Carolyn laughed softly as Nathan raised surprised brows in Nick's direction, the dark-haired man lounging in an armchair, completely unperturbed by his fiancée's flirtatious manner. 'Don't worry, Nathan, Nick isn't likely to challenge you to a duel or anything just because I like the way you look. Just because we're getting married there's no reason to act as if we don't see the attraction of other people.'

Brenna was well aware of Carolyn's views concerning her engagement, just as she was also aware that Carolyn had been faithful to Nick and the love they shared, since the moment they first met. But Nathan couldn't know that from the way Carolyn was acting, and Brenna could sense his sceptical gaze on her.

'Carolyn is the author of *Koly the Koala*,' she defensively explained her friendship with the other woman; the two of them had been introduced through the publisher almost a year ago. 'We're currently working on another book together,' she added protectively as she could still feel the sting of his contempt for the arrangement he thought Carolyn and Nick had, obviously considering her part of their relationship at the moment.

'How nice,' he drawled uninterestedly, managing to extricate himself from Carolyn's languidly dangling arm before moving to stand in front of the window. 'If you would like to pack your things, Brenna,' he added hardly, 'we can be on our way.'

'I'll help you,' offered Carolyn with a generosity uncharacteristic of her, almost pushing Brenna from the room and up the narrow stairs to the two bedrooms and bathroom above. Brenna had one of the bedrooms, Carolyn and Nick shared the other one. 'Where are you going with that delicious hunk of a man?' Carolyn demanded to know as soon as the bedroom door closed behind them, making herself comfortable on the bed as Brenna ruefully began to pack.

'That "delicious hunk of a man" is merely my stepbrother——'

'Nathan Wade has never been *merely* anything in his life,' her friend dismissed knowingly. 'I can't believe you haven't noticed how handsome he is,' she chided. 'After all, your stepbrother is no relation.'

It would be useless to deny that she hadn't been aware of Nathan's masculinely magnetic pull from the time she had first met him; there had been a constant and steady stream of women in his life the last ten years to testify to that even if she hadn't been aware of it.

'When someone has watched you progress through braces on your teeth, pimples, braids, and a flat chest, there doesn't seem any place left for romance,' she avoided drily.

'I would have made sure he noticed the disappearance of the braids, the brace and the

pimples, and the appearance of my breasts,'
Carolyn told her enviously. 'We would probably
have been sharing a bed by the time I reached
seventeen!'

Brenna didn't doubt that, and smiled affec-
tionately at her friend. Before she met Nick,
Carolyn had known a lot of other men, she was a
woman that men seemed to like instinctively.
Except Nathan, she realised frowningly. Probably
her friends *weren't* good enough for him!

'I was still wearing the brace at seventeen,' she
dismissed scornfully.

'But surely ... Oh, never mind,' Carolyn
sighed frustratedly at Brenna's closed expression.
'Where's he taking you?'

'London. I ... He and my sister decided to pay
me a surprise visit and I ruined it by not being
there.' She had no intention of discussing this
family crisis with Carolyn, considering it too
personal. 'She's waiting in London for me.'
Which was true—she hoped!

'Your sister came over with Nathan?' Carolyn
frowned. 'But I thought she was married to
someone called Grant? Why ...?'

'She is. Look, I really don't have the time to
talk right now, Carolyn,' Brenna cut in briskly. 'I
have to get my packing done; Nathan doesn't like
to be kept waiting,' she added truthfully,
remembering a couple of times he had been
waiting up for her when she arrived home later
from a date than she had said she would. And she
could do without his chilly sarcasm in front of
her friends!

Carolyn stood up in a graceful movement, sighing her disappointment. 'You're really no fun when it comes to confidences, Brenna,' she complained. 'I've told you all about my life before I met Nick.'

And some of it had made her toes curl! But she liked Carolyn, and the two of them worked very well together, she just had no intention of discussing her complicated family tree, and the problems her mother's marriage to Patrick Wade had made for all concerned.

'Maybe when I get back.'

'How long will you be gone?' Carolyn was completely professional now, the deadline for the book being only weeks away.

Brenna grimaced. 'I'm really not sure.' Everything depended on whether or not Lesli came to her, and what her sister decided to do then.

'Call me as soon as you know,' Carolyn instructed as she made her way out of the room. 'We're really on a tight schedule.'

She knew that, it was the reason they had sought the peace and privacy of this out-of-the-way cottage. But if Carolyn and Nick hadn't disappeared to Florida for the month of July they wouldn't have had this problem.

But she didn't argue that point, but nodded abruptly, concentrating on getting her cases packed so that she and Nathan could leave.

Carolyn had prepared a tray of coffee during Brenna's absence—it had to be coffee, Nathan didn't drink tea!—as the three of them sat together in the lounge. Nathan looked very relaxed as he lounged in his chair, his jacket casually flung over the back of it, as if he had no intention of giving it up in case it got lost in the clutter that Carolyn surrounded herself with wherever she went. Brenna anxiously searched their faces, deciding that Nathan looked the most relaxed—and wondering what he had said or done to put that wary look in the eyes of the other couple. He returned her accusing look with bland indifference to her discomfort.

She said hasty goodbyes to Carolyn and Nick while Nathan put her luggage in the back of the sleek car he had hired, its smooth compact lines telling of its exclusive nameplate. She barely waited before they were down the lane and out on to the road before turning on him. 'Well?' she demanded.

He shot her a cursory glance before turning back to the road. 'Well what?' he drawled unhelpfully.

'What did you say to them?' Her eyes were narrowed suspiciously.

He shrugged. 'We barely spoke while you were upstairs packing.'

'*What did you say to them?*'

'Calm down, Brenna,' he advised impatiently.

'I am calm,' she ground out. 'I just want to know what you said to upset my friends.'

'They weren't upset.'

'Nathan!'

He gave a weary sigh. 'I merely expressed regret for breaking up your *ménage à trois*. That is the fashionable description for what you were doing, isn't it?' he added harshly.

Strangely the insult made her feel like crying rather than shouting. That Nathan could think she had changed so much as to be involved in anything so distasteful! She had been a virgin when they made love, did he really think she could have become such a wanton in the last year?

'Maybe I shouldn't have made love to you when I did.' The same memories seemed to be going through his mind, making his expression grim. 'If I hadn't maybe you wouldn't have felt free to experiment with other men.'

There had been no other men. She wasn't stupid, she knew that what she and Nathan had shared that last night in Canada had been unique, unmatchable with any other man. She knew that just as surely as she recognised that, for her own sanity, it could never be repeated. *Never*, she vowed with a shudder. It had taken her months to accept that she and Nathan had made love. And she wasn't going to let herself fall into the same trap her mother and Lesli had.

'Brenna?'

She flinched as he would have touched her, moving as far away from him as she could.

'What the hell!' Nathan's face darkened like a thunder-cloud as he turned to look at her. 'Brenna, what is it?' He frowned at how pale she had become.

'What is it?' she repeated haltingly, still very disturbed. 'It isn't every day I'm accused of being a whore!'

'I never called you that!' he rasped.

'As good as.' She flushed in her anger.

He gave a deep, ragged sigh. 'Okay, what was your relationship to those two?'

'I told you, Carolyn writes the books, and I illustrate them.'

'And Nick Bancroft?'

'Shares Carolyn's room,' she told him resentfully. 'The two of them go everywhere together.'

'That wasn't the impression I got,' Nathan bit out contemptuously.

'Appearances can be deceptive.' Although Carolyn had been very sexually active before meeting and falling in love with Nick, to her knowledge, for all her friend's talk, Carolyn had been faithful to him since they first fell in love. The habit of flirting with every man she met was obviously a hard one for Carolyn to break. 'Carolyn writes children's books, not sex manuals!'

'Okay,' Nathan sighed. 'If I was wrong, I'm sorry.'

The words were so quietly spoken Brenna couldn't help wondering if she had imagined them; Nathan never apologised for anything, none of the Wade men did. But this time Nathan had, she could tell that by the angry set of his mouth, the stiff way he sat behind the wheel of the car, as if he deeply resented having to apologise. And Brenna was sure that he did.

She neither accepted nor denied the apology, turning so that she was looking out of the side window, her face stiffly averted all the way back to London.

It was late afternoon by the time they reached London and the top floor of the Victorian building which Brenna occupied, one of the rooms having been converted into a studio for her, the light up there being excellent for her work. She had lived in the flat only a year, moving from the one she had shared with two other girls through college, so that Nathan shouldn't find her if he came looking. It seemed she could have saved herself the trouble, she thought ruefully; Nathan didn't give a damn about reading other people's personal mail to obtain what he wanted.

He carried her two suitcases up the six flights of stairs, putting them down outside her door while Brenna searched for her key in her bag.

She turned to him. 'If you tell me the name of your hotel I'll call you if I hear from Lesli——'

'I booked out of my hotel this morning.' Nathan took the key out of her hand and deftly turned it in the lock. 'If Lesli calls or comes here, I'll be waiting for her.' He gently urged Brenna inside the flat before he followed with the two suitcases.

'Here?' Brenna finally managed to gasp. 'You mean *here*?' She came to an abrupt halt just inside the lounge when she saw the brown suitcase standing in the middle of the room. 'Yours?' she squeaked at Nathan.

His mouth quirked. 'When I explained to your landlady that I'm your brother, and flashed Lesli's

and Grant's wedding photograph at her with the
four of us standing together, she was kind enough
to unlock your door and let me leave my case
here. So you see, Brenna, I'm here for the
duration.'

CHAPTER TWO

BRENNA'S eyes shot sparks at Nathan's arrogance, his downright nerve in daring to assume he could do such a thing. 'I don't care what you told Mrs Marlow, you are not staying here!' she told him furiously. 'You had no right to have your case put here under false pretences. I ought to telephone the police.'

'And tell them what? I am your brother——'

'Like hell you are! You——'

'Brenna,' Nathan's voice was soft, dangerously so, 'what did I do the last time you swore at me?'

An embarrassed blush darkened her cheeks as she remembered how painful a certain part of her anatomy had been the time she had called him an arrogant bastard. She hadn't been able to sit down comfortably for a week!

'I'm glad the memory is still with you,' he drawled, carrying her cases through to her bedroom without the least sign of hesitation. His mouth quirked in amusement as he came back to find her glaring at him accusingly. 'I had a look round this morning,' he mocked.

'Checking to see if I had a live-in lover?' she snapped resentfully.

He shrugged. 'I was just curious about where you had been living since you left college. I wasn't aware that an illustrator was paid enough

to afford a place like this.' He sat down uninvited
in an armchair, stretching his long legs out in
front of him as he turned to arch one eyebrow
questioningly at her.

Brenna's mouth firmed. Although this was an
attic flat she did occupy the whole floor, three
smaller flats on each of the two lower floors, and
he was right in his assumption; the rent on this
place each month cost her a small fortune.

'Don't tell me,' he drawled mockingly, 'that
you've forgotten all your avowals to the contrary
and spent some of the Wade money?'

She drew in a shaky breath, hating to have to
make the admission. When their parents had died
she had been shocked to learn that Patrick had
left everything equally among the four children,
had been stunned that he hadn't made the
distinction between his own children and his
second wife's. But neither Nathan or Grant had
questioned it, and Brenna had known why; she
had known that the money, and Lesli's and her
own share of the Wade ranch, was just a pay-off
for a guilty conscience from a man who had
believed money could atone for all sins. Brenna
had known exactly what it was, and refused to
accept any of it. But last year when she left
college she had had no choice. But as soon as she
began to earn money on her illustrating she was
going to pay the money back she had borrowed
with interest, and had no intention of taking
anything from the Wades.

'I'm going to pay it back,' she snapped.

'For God's sake, Brenna——'

'You can't stay here, Nathan.' She turned away.

'Then you do have a live-in lover?' he taunted.

'No—and I don't want one either!' she glared at him pointedly.

'Pity,' he drawled. 'Still, I did notice a cot-bed in the studio when I looked around this morning, I'm sure I'll be comfortable on that.'

'There are no curtains at the windows!' she protested.

'Then I guess I'll have to go out and buy some pyjamas, won't I?' he reasoned.

'Nathan——'

'Brenna?' He arched forbidding black brows.

'Nathan, you know it wouldn't be right for you to stay here,' she choked almost pleadingly, knowing she was going to hate herself for the weakness later but not caring at that moment.

His eyes became icy. 'As you so rightly said earlier, Brenna, that's over,' he dismissed harshly. 'I'm here to find Lesli; I'm not going to attempt to touch you. You can trust me, Brenna,' he sighed at her apprehensive expression.

But could she trust herself? She had wanted this man again ever since that night in his arms, and it wasn't to be. It *couldn't* be! 'I'll go down and ask Mrs Marlow if Lesli has been here,' she said dully.

'Does that mean I can stay?' he asked softly.

'Did I ever have any choice?' she rasped.

'You know I've never used force on you,' Nathan said quietly.

Because he had never needed to, not when it

came to the important things. Oh, she fought him over everything, but when it came to the crunch, Nathan always won the battles he really wanted to, and as he said, always without the use of force. Sixteen months ago she had been afraid of committing herself to the domination of his arrogance, and after speaking to her father on her return to England she had been glad of that hesitation. It had saved her from making a mistake that would have surely destroyed her.

Mrs Marlow was a small bird-like woman, always avid to know all that she could about her seven boarders; she was obviously desperate for information about the man with the North American accent who claimed to be Brenna's brother!

'I hope I did the right thing, dear,' she spoke curiously. 'He sounded so convincing.'

Brenna couldn't help wondering, a little cynically, if some of that 'convincing' hadn't been in a monetary form. The Wades had shown more than once that they believed everyone and everything had its price, and Mrs Marlow wasn't the type to take anyone's word for anything that they claimed to be.

'Nathan is my stepbrother,' she dismissed briskly. 'Have I had any other visitors during the last few days?' She frowned, her worry over Lesli paramount. She couldn't think what could have been serious enough for Grant and Lesli to argue about to make her sister walk out on her husband. The two of them had their ups and downs like most married couples, but never like this before. And with the birth of the baby being so close all this couldn't be doing Lesli any good.

'Wasn't Mr Wade enough?' the middle-aged woman twittered, habitually fingering the pearls about her throat, the smoky jewels given a pink tinge from the deep rose-coloured blouse she wore tucked neatly into the waistband of her black cotton skirt. 'How exciting to have a visitor come all that way just to see you!'

Brenna doubted very much that she would find the occurrence exciting even if Nathan had come here specifically to see her. At least, not in the way Mrs Marlow meant!

'There's no trouble at home, is there, dear?' the other woman frowned. 'Only I couldn't help noticing Mr Wade seemed a little—disturbed, when he was here this morning.'

'No trouble, Mrs Marlow,' Brenna said firmly, having no intention of satisfying this woman's curiosity either. 'So I've had no other visitors?' she persisted, knowing the other woman would keep her chatting here all day while she waited for her answer.

'No, dear,' the landlady smiled. 'But I have your mail here,' she picked up the dozen or so letters from the hall table behind her and handed them to Brenna.

Brenna could hardly conceal her disappointment at the other woman's negative answer, and absently made her parting as she slowly went back up the stairs, idly flicking through the letters in her hand. Her heart skipped a beat as she reached an envelope written in her sister's handwriting, only to be closely followed by renewed disappointment when she saw the date of the Canadian postmark; Lesli had written the letter long before her departure from the Wade ranch.

Nevertheless, she ripped open the envelope, hoping to find some hint of her sister's emotional state. The letter was as newsy as always, telling of a new bull Grant had acquired, how hot she was finding it this summer with the added weight of the baby to carry around, how she and Mindy, the Wade housekeeper, had prepared the nursery before Lesli became too big to help. As usual there was no mention of Nathan, as there hadn't been from the moment Brenna had made it clear she had no interest in knowing of Nathan's movements. The last year of complete silence about him had been very hard to bear, but she hadn't dared let herself think about him, let alone of the latest woman he was dating. She had no doubt that Lesli would break the silence if Nathan should announce his intention of getting married! She never had.

And now Nathan was here, upstairs in her flat. God, how it had pained her to turn and face him earlier today. But she had done it! She was proud of herself, of the way she had handled the meeting she had known would be inevitable on the birth of Lesli and Grant's baby. It had shook her that it had come two months earlier than she had expected, that was all.

She could do this, she could get through seeing Nathan, being with him again. She had better!

'Anything?' Nathan put his hand over the mouthpiece of the telephone as Brenna let herself in, obviously in the middle of a call.

She shook her head, frowning. 'If that's Grant I want to talk to him before you ring off,' she told him firmly.

'I——' Nathan flashed her an irritated look as he was obviously questioned as to his attentiveness down the line. 'Yes. Yes, I'm still here,' he bit out tersely. 'Of course I'll pass your message on,' he assured the caller smoothly before putting down the receiver.

'I told you——'

'It wasn't Grant,' he drawled softly, challengingly.

Brenna's eyes narrowed. 'Who?' she demanded abruptly, slightly irked that he should have taken a call obviously meant for her.

'Your friend Carolyn. Apparently you packed one of Nick's favourite T-shirts in with your things today.'

Colour flared in her cheeks at his contemptuous expression. 'I was using it to sleep in,' she defended hotly. 'I forgot to leave it behind.'

Dark brows rose sceptically. 'As I recall, you never used to bother with nightclothes,' Nathan drawled.

Her mouth tightened as she recalled the time he had walked into her bedroom to invite her for an early morning swim, laughingly pulling back the bedclothes as she snuggled down in their depths as a refusal. For long timeless minutes he had stood looking down at her, and she had seen the beauty he found in her body reflected in his eyes before he snarled something about going on his own and slammed out of the room. After that she had always made sure her bedroom door was locked, not being prepared to change her sleeping habits on the off chance that he might invade her room again.

'I still don't,' she snapped. 'But that could have proved a little awkward if Nick and I had met on the way to the bathroom!'

'And you think the man's T-shirt was preferable?' Nathan rasped angrily.

'Carolyn doesn't wear nightclothes either!'

'No, I can believe that,' he dismissed impatiently. 'I find it very difficult to believe she wrote a children's book!' he added scathingly.

'And just what do you really know about her?' Brenna challenged. 'Do you have any idea *why* she behaves the way that she does? What made her come on to you even in front of Nick?'

He sighed wearily, dropping down into an armchair, his left ankle resting on his right knee as he relaxed back against the brown material. 'I'm sure you're going to tell me,' he drawled uninterestedly.

'God, you're so damned smug, sitting there behind your Wade name and your Wade wealth——'

'I thought we were talking about Carolyn Frank,' he cut in flintily, his whole body tensed now.

'We are,' she confirmed tersely. 'Carolyn lived in foster-homes from the time she was six days old until she reached sixteen and got a job—that's also how she became so adept at weaving children's stories, by telling them to all her little "brothers and sisters",' she bit out. 'Even her name isn't her own, not really,' she gave a pained frown. 'There was a note pinned on her saying her mother's name was Carolyn and her father's name was Frank, and as they were both only fifteen they couldn't care for her properly. The young mother also begged for the baby not to be adopted, promised she would come back for her one day.'

'But she never did,' Nathan rasped flatly.

'No,' she said abruptly.

'And ever since Carolyn has done everything she can to make people like her, as a salve to her mother's desertion,' he guessed huskily. 'I had no idea.'

'How could you?' Brenna couldn't forgive his contempt and condescension so easily, she had been at the receiving end of it herself for too long to do that. 'You just looked at her and saw a flirtatious butterfly, you didn't stop to ask *why* she's like that——'

'For God's sake, Brenna,' he snapped abruptly, 'I only met the woman for a matter of minutes!'

'Long enough to have passed judgment on her, obviously!'

'I've said I was sorry,' he sighed. 'What more can I do?'

'Stop standing up as judge and jury on me and the people I call friends,' she said in exasperation.

'You were my sister for nine years, Brenna,

and I thought I was going to marry you for three months; I can't shut off my protectiveness towards you just because you order it!' His voice rose angrily.

'I never asked for it in the first place,' she dismissed contemptuously.

'That's like saying you didn't ask the sun to set,' he sneered. 'It was just as inevitable.'

'I don't see why, you virtually ignored me until I was sixteen!'

'I'm not going to even bother to answer that accusation, I think it speaks for itself,' he drawled mockingly.

'Isn't that just typical!' she scorned. 'I wasn't *worth* noticing until I started to look like a woman.'

'Oh, for God's sake, Brenna,' Nathan stood up forcibly. 'Next you'll be coming out with that hackneyed male chauvinist pig line.' He thrust his hands into the pockets of his trousers, pulling the material taut. 'You were a damned little pest until you were sixteen, and it had nothing to do with being a woman. You arrived in Canada resenting everyone and everything connected with your mother's remarriage. Never mind that she was happy, you weren't, and you had no intention of being so in the near future either. Most young girls would have felt some excitement mixed in with their trepidation at moving to a new and vast country, of having two older brothers to suddenly grant their every wish——'

'Sitting me on top of a ten-foot horse wasn't my wish!' Brenna still shuddered at the memory of her first experience on a horse's back. Grant had swung her up on top of the horse her second day in Canada, finding it incredible when she had protested she had never ridden before. He had finally taken pity on her and lifted her down, but it had taken months for her to get up on one again.

'Grant was only trying to treat you like his baby sister,' Nathan scowled. 'How was he to know you had lived in a town all your life and hardly knew what a horse looked like, let alone ridden one!'

'He could have asked! Besides, we might not have been told of your existence before we arrived there, but I would have thought your father would have told you about Lesli and me.'

'Until my father announced his intention of marrying your mother and bringing her back to Canada with him we had no idea of either her existence or yours,' he dismissed. 'Why should we?'

Why indeed? Why should the arrogant Wade brothers care that their equally arrogant father had walked into a family unit and smashed it to pieces? Without Patrick Wade's interference her parents might have smoothed out their problems and made a success of their marriage. But not once Patrick Wade had decided otherwise.

Not that she had disliked her stepfather, not then anyway. She had just found the grand way that he lived, his wealth and power, very intimidating. No, the dislike had come later, much later.

'Don't you think we should telephone Grant now?' she suggested waspishly. 'After all, he just might be worried.'

Sarcasm dripped from the caustically spoken words, and Nathan's eyes flashed like pinpoints of silver. 'Why did I never notice before what a vicious little bitch you can be?' he snapped.

Brenna blushed angrily at his contempt. 'You noticed, Nathan,' she ground out. 'You even liked it on occasion,' she reminded him coldly, that night in his arms, long hours of fiery, driven passion, forever imprinted in her mind and senses.

His mouth twisted. 'I should have remembered I liked you better when you're purring like a kitten and not spitting like a cat.'

'Could we get this call to Grant over?' she snapped. 'I'd like to start calling some of the less than major hotels to see if Lesli is staying at one of them. You did realise there were other hotels in London besides the Savoy, the Hilton, the Dorchester——'

'Cut the damned sarcasm, Brenna,' he rasped. 'It isn't achieving anything.'

It wasn't even giving her that much satisfaction; arguing with Nathan never had. Even when she was sure she had emerged the victor from one of their heated exchanges she always felt the loser!

She briskly put the call through to Grant, slightly disconcerted when the receiver was picked up the other end after only the second ring. 'Grant?' she began.

'Lesli?' he returned sharply. 'God, Lesli, where are you?'

'It's Brenna, Grant,' she interrupted gently, her fears as to Grant's worry for his wife's safety firmly put to rest; he sounded like a desperately unhappy man.

'Oh.' He bit back his disappointment. 'Sorry. Your voices have always sounded the same over the telephone.'

'She hasn't come home?' she prompted softly.

'No,' he rasped. 'God, how I wish I hadn't let Nathan talk me into letting him be the one to go to London; I'm going insane just sitting here waiting for news,' he groaned. 'Is Nathan with you now?'

She glanced over to where Nathan sat stiffly forward in his chair. 'Yes, he's here,' she confirmed abruptly. 'Grant, Lesli hasn't contacted me at all,' she told him as gently as she could.

'Where can she be?' he groaned.

'Grant, what did the two of you argue about to make her do something like this?'

'I think that's between Lesli and me,' he answered hardly.

'I realise that. But——'

'Can I talk to Nathan?' he cut in tersely.

She gave a frustrated sigh. 'Of course,' she snapped, holding out the receiver to Nathan. 'He wants to talk to his big brother.' She still felt stung by Grant's refusal to confide in her.

Nathan looked at her contemptuously. 'Maybe instead of trying to make you feel welcome ten years ago we should have put you over our knees a few times,' he bit out harshly. 'Come to think of it, it's still not too late to do that.'

She knew the undue haste in which she handed him the receiver and moved to the other side of the room smacked of running away from him, but over the years Nathan had proved to be a man who carried out his threats.

Where could Lesli be? Nathan's taunt about her and Lesli sticking together was a true one. She and Lesli had always been close, even more so after they were uprooted and taken to Canada; she couldn't believe her sister wouldn't come to her or contact her soon.

'—and I'm staying on here with Brenna until she hears from Lesli,' she came back in on Nathan's telephone conversation to hear him assure his younger brother.

Earlier she had reluctantly agreed to let him stay here with her until they heard from Lesli, but now she wondered just how long that was going to be. Lesli had left the ranch three days ago, and she hadn't contacted any of them yet. And Nathan couldn't stay here at the flat with her indefinitely.

'Keep in touch,' Nathan added abruptly before ringing off, turning to Brenna with cold eyes. 'Your sister seems as adept at disappearing as you are,' he bit out.

Her mouth firmed as she realised he was referring to the way she had moved out of the flat she had shared a year ago, making it impossible for him to find her even if he had wanted to. She had never found out if he had wanted to.

She looked at Nathan with dislike. 'I'm sure both of us had good reason for disappearing; I know *I* did,' she bit out tautly.

His eyes narrowed. 'I'd be interested to hear it.'

'Surely it's obvious?' she challenged contemptuously. 'The thought of marrying you is enough for any woman to want to make herself scarce!'

'You didn't feel that way the night you spent in my bed!' he grated.

Her cheeks were deathly pale. 'It was *my* bed,' she clarified that he was the one who had come to her. 'And surely it's obvious I mean to imply that I must have been slightly deranged that night?'

Nathan looked at her coldly in that still way of his that had always unnerved her, and to her chagrin Brenna was the first to look away. She hadn't been deranged that night, she *had* been slightly intoxicated, but she had a feeling they both knew she wasn't intoxicated enough not to have known what she was doing when she invited Nathan to her room.

'I'll go and make up the bed in the studio for you,' she mumbled.

He nodded abruptly. 'And I'll go out and buy those pyjamas,' he jeered.

Brenna sat down heavily once he had left, not sure who had won that last argument. If anyone had! There was really no point in arguing about the fact that she had decided against marrying him; she had never said that she would, and they both knew that too! For a while, for the space of a single night, she had allowed herself the luxury of dropping the guard of bitterness she felt towards all the Wade family, for the space of that one night she and Nathan had seduced each other into believing they actually cared about each other. At least, she had allowed herself to be seduced; despite what Nathan had said to the contrary his motives had been much more basic.

His mention of marriage had unnerved her into agreeing to consider the possibility once she had finished college in the summer. And if her father hadn't re-instilled some of the Jordan pride in her she just might have done that. She was grateful for her lucky escape.

The cot-bed was made and a snack dinner partly prepared by the time Nathan knocked on the door just over an hour later. Brenna answered it, her denims and T-shirt replaced with a purple lounge dress.

'Are we dressing or *undressing* for dinner?' Nathan drawled as he walked past her.

Brenna paused at the door, willing her temper to remain under control. She should be used to Nathan's caustic tongue by now, she had been listening to it long enough! Besides, the dress was perfectly respectable, even if the softness of the material did more than flatter her curves. She always changed into something loose and comfortable during her evenings at home, and she wasn't about to change her routine for this man.

He had thrown his paper-bag-wrapped parcel into a chair, had taken off his jacket and was loosening the buttons on his shirt by the time she joined him. Her senses baulked at the sight of his tanned, hair-roughened, muscular chest, knowing there was a slight scar just below his left nipple, from a childhood accident. She willed her expression to remain bland as she remembered caressing that scar, and above it, the night in his arms.

'What are we having for dinner?' he drawled. 'Bean sprouts and carrot fritters?'

He certainly wasn't making it easy to be polite to him! 'We're having omelettes—cheese or mushroom, whichever you prefer, with salad and baked potato. And there's fruit to follow. It's all I could get together at such short notice.'

'Sounds good. Better than the last time you fed me, anyway,' he grinned. 'Whoever heard of a girl brought up on a ranch being a vegetarian!'

Brenna's eyes flashed deeply green. 'I wasn't brought up on a ranch, I was transplanted to one at an age when I could realise those lovely little calves born in the spring would ultimately be fattened up to be sent for slaughter!' She shuddered at those childhood memories. 'It isn't that I don't like meat, I'm as carnivorous as the next person, I just feel nauseous every time I think of some poor animal being murdered so that I can eat something I don't *need* in the first place! We don't need to eat cows, we can live just as well on the things they produce, the same goes for fowl, and sheep provide wool to keep us warm. We don't have to *eat* the poor creatures.'

'Get off your soap-box, Brenna,' Nathan ran a tired hand over his eyes. 'I've heard it all before. Ranching is what I do for a living.'

'That's probably what all those whalers say!'

He gave an impatient sigh. 'There's no

connection between the destruction of the whale and my ranching a few cows.'

'It's thousands of cows,' she corrected fiercely. 'And the connection they both have is that they die for man's gain. You——'

'Could we have our omelettes—make mine cheese,' he ground out. 'It's been a long day, and I can do without this old argument. You don't accept the money that's due to you from the ranch because of your beliefs, and I respect that, but I don't expect to get lectures every time we see each other.'

The fact that she abhorred the slaughter of those beautiful animals that lived such a short time was only part of the reason Brenna had refused the Wade money, and the fact that Nathan had never realised that was just part of his insensitivity.

'I'm sure you know where the shower is if you would like to freshen up before dinner,' she suggested distantly. 'The food will be ready in about fifteen minutes.'

'Thanks.' He picked up his parcel and carried it through to the studio, emerging a few minutes later with fresh clothes and accurately locating the shower; obviously he had found that too when he 'looked around this morning'!

It was amazing how much more sensually Nathan's faded denims seemed to mould to him, how much more blatantly masculine he looked, with the top three buttons of his shirt undone as they usually were, here in her small fitted kitchen. They were things she had barely been aware of her years in Canada, but here he had the look of a caged tiger, and she knew he was as dangerous.

'You didn't have any luck with the less than major hotels, I take it?' he drawled before biting crisply into an apple after their meal.

'No,' she muttered, having been hoping her own lack of success in locating Lesli would go unquestioned, but having known that it wouldn't.

'What a pity. And you were so certain too!' he mocked.

'Nathan——'

'Shall we clear away?' he suggested briskly. 'The last couple of days have seemed like a week, and I'd like to get some sleep now. When you Jordan women decide to run off you make sure it disturbs as many lives as possible, don't you?' he bit out hardly.

'I'm sure you'll find Lesli has a very good reason for acting this way.'

'So you've already said,' he nodded, giving a wry grimace. 'But as Grant isn't in a talkative mood right now, and Lesli probably won't be any more forthcoming when she turns up, we may never know what it was.'

'As long as they sort out this mess and get back together it's none of our business,' Brenna dismissed shruggingly. 'No matter what you may think I don't want their marriage to break up. They love each other.'

'Yes,' Nathan sighed. 'I wonder why so many people bother with the emotion, it seems a painful one to me.'

'I can clear away these few things if you would like to go to bed,' she said abruptly. 'Although it's still light outside, and with no curtains . . .' she added doubtfully.

'Have you forgotten you're talking to the man who fell asleep on horseback in the middle of the day?' he drawled drily.

'Oh, yes,' her mouth quirked. 'Patrick really laid into you for that, didn't he?' she chuckled.

'He sure did.' Nathan's eyes were warm with the memory.

'What was it he accused you of?' she mused mischievously. '"Whoring all night with——"'

'You shouldn't have been listening to that, young lady,' he grimaced.

'The whole ranch must have heard it,' she grinned. 'At that age I wasn't quite sure what he meant——'

'You shouldn't have even half understood it,' Nathan glowered.

'Maybe I wouldn't have done if you hadn't shouted right back that it was your business and no one else's who you went to bed with, and——'

'I remember the rest of it, thank you,' Nathan grimaced again.

'I never thought you were an innocent, Nathan,' she taunted.

'All the same——'

'Go to bed, Nathan,' she mocked. 'If I hear from Lesli I'll let you know.'

'Will you?' he looked at her with narrowed eyes.

She sighed. 'Yes.'

'Brenna . . .'

She neatly avoided his reaching hands. 'Will you just go to bed?' she said tautly.

His eyes had narrowed to icy slits. 'You needn't be afraid of me,' he rasped. 'I answered an invitation when I came to your room sixteen months ago, I wouldn't do it again unless the same invitation were made. You're perfectly safe from me tonight.'

Her gaze remained steady in the face of his derision. 'Good night, Nathan.'

She was very much aware of him in the adjoining room as she prepared for bed, and she knew he was right when he said she had given the invitation that night. They had all been to a party at a neighbour's ranch the last night of her Easter break from college, and Nathan had been her partner for the evening. After years of treating him as an older brother she didn't particularly like, she had become sharply aware of his masculinity as they danced together. She hadn't wanted to be aware of him as anything other than one of the arrogant Wades, who bought people as they did their livestock, but the wine she had consumed had put a hazy red glow around the evening, so that by the time they drove home her head was resting on Nathan's shoulder as he sat behind the wheel.

Lesli and Grant had made their excuses without seeming to notice Nathan and Brenna's absorption with each other, the married couple having eyes only for each other.

'We may as well go to bed too,' Brenna had said throatily, her gaze held by his.

'Yours or mine?' he said, half teasingly, and yet half seriously too.

She felt as if she stood on a precipice at that moment, wanting the treasure she was sure was just beyond the edge. 'Mine,' she said recklessly.

Nathan was no inexperienced teenager to match her, but the surprise of her answer had obviously unnerved him, for he swallowed hard. 'Ten minutes?' he suggested gruffly.

'Make it five,' she taunted, laughingly running to her room.

She had felt lightheaded and happy, singing in the shower, curled up like a sensuous kitten by the time Nathan quietly knocked on the door and entered her room, the belted towelling robe obviously his only clothing.

'Why don't you slip into something more comfortable?' she teased. 'Skin!'

She had been wrong, the towelling robe wasn't his only clothing; black briefs clung to the perfection of his thighs.

'Those too,' she encouraged huskily.

'Are you going to regret this in the morning?' he frowned his hesitation.

'Probably,' she dismissed. 'But what's that saying, "Tomorrow is another day"?'

Still he hesitated, a golden god bathed in the lamp's warm glow. 'Are you going to hate me?'

'More than I already do, you mean?' she giggled.

'Brenna——'

'If you question all your women like this before you make love to them I'm surprised you've had any lovers at all,' she pouted, provocatively letting the sheet fall down to her waist as she sat up, her breasts thrusting forward in rose-tipped invitation.

And she knew exactly what she was doing; she felt like a stranger apart from herself watching her actions, unable to stop what was about to happen.

'This is different, Brenna——'

'Why?' she mocked. 'Because of who I am? Forget about that, Nathan. For goodness' sake,' she snapped impatiently. 'If you aren't interested, there were a dozen men at the party tonight who were!'

'I'm well aware of that,' he grated, discarding the black scrap of material before joining her beneath the bedclothes. 'You're like a witch, Brenna, casting your spells over every man you meet,' he groaned. 'In fact, you're probably descended from one!' His mouth claimed hers, and Brenna became lost in the whirlpool of emotions that was Nathan Wade.

No part of her remained bereft of his touch, and she writhed beneath him in ecstasy as his tongue rasped across the turgid peaks of her breasts, her legs becoming entangled with his as she arched into him.

But as in everything else, Nathan took his time making love, bringing her again and again to a peak of pleasure before denying her the full glory of it, until in self-defence she began an assault on his senses that soon made him gasp as his body leapt out of control.

'No, not too fast,' he groaned as he pulled her above him. 'God knows I've waited long enough!' he muttered raggedly. 'Brenna, have you . . . will this be the first time for you?' he frowned up at her.

'Do we have to bother with details?' she dismissed impatiently, nipping at his chest with her teeth.

'They aren't details, you silly girl. There could be a child——'

'A baby?' she realised in a puzzled voice. 'Don't be silly,' she said scornfully.

'God, Brenna, you have to know that it wouldn't bother me if you did become pregnant; I'd like to have a child with you,' he rasped huskily. 'How I love you! Will you marry me?'

'Marry you?' she blinked dazedly.

'Yes.' He rolled over until she was beneath him, cupping each side of her face with his gentle hands as his thighs parted hers, catching her pained gasp in his mouth as his lips met hers the same time as he gently stroked her.

She couldn't think, let alone answer him, and it was a long time later, with her cheek resting against his damp chest, that he returned to the subject of marriage.

'Are you going to marry me, witch?' He absently played with the tangle of her hair as it lay down her spine.

Sobering up could be a hard lesson, in more ways than one, and Brenna shied from committing herself to the son of a man who took everything he wanted as if it were his right, knowing Patrick

Wade had brought up his two sons to believe the same was true of them.

'I still have to finish college,' she evaded.

'And I wouldn't dream of trying to stop you, a few more months isn't going to make that much difference,' Nathan said indulgently.

'Then could we wait until I come home for good before we make any decisions?'

'Of course,' he murmured, desire flooding back into his body 'Just remember, I love you.'

He had made love to her all through the night, and Brenna had been exhausted when she said goodbye to him at the airport the next day, too weary to do more than sleep on the long flight back to London. Although she knew she had to seriously consider her actions of the night before, to try and work out what had possessed her to invite Nathan to her bed.

But in the end she hadn't needed to think about that or Nathan's proposal. Her father had met her at the airport, a broken replica of the happy-go-lucky man she remembered from her childhood. And she knew it was the Wades who had so destroyed him; she hadn't needed to be reminded of that as he drank his way through a bottle of whisky before telling her about his visit to the doctor that morning.

CHAPTER THREE

THE ringing of the telephone woke Brenna the next morning—afternoon, she corrected with a groan as she looked at the bedside clock to find it was almost twelve o'clock. Why didn't Nathan answer the damned thing?—he was always up at six o'clock, no matter what the circumstances.

It was on about the eighth ring that she realised he couldn't be in the flat, otherwise he would have answered the telephone, so she crawled out of her double bed to answer it herself, pulling on Nick's T-shirt that almost reached down to her knees to pick up the receiver and groggily recite her number.

'You really shouldn't do that in London,' Carolyn instantly chided. 'It could be an obscene telephone caller.'

'They wouldn't dare, not with Nathan here,' retorted Brenna.

'I don't suppose your exhaustion could be due to your handsome stepbrother?' Carolyn suggested hopefully.

'No,' she denied drily. At least, not in the way her friend meant; once those memories of Nathan that last night in Canada had been evoked she hadn't been able to get them out of her mind, and it had been almost morning before she fell asleep.

'Pity,' her friend sighed. 'Is he there?'

'He doesn't seem to be ... wait a minute,' Brenna turned the telephone pad around to face her, reading the large masculine scrawl on its surface. 'He's out,' she sighed.

'Damn,' muttered Carolyn. 'I wanted to thank him for the flowers.'

'What flowers?' she frowned, sleep still fogging her brain.

'The ones he sent me, silly,' her friend laughed. 'A dozen long-stemmed white roses,' she added delightedly.

The fog at last cleared from Brenna's brain as she realised the reason Nathan had sent the flowers. It wasn't a gesture she would have expected from him, but she thanked him for his thoughtfulness anyway.

'To apologise for his rudeness yesterday, the card with them said,' Carolyn continued, very often not needing answers to her conversation, just taking the answers for granted. 'I didn't particularly think he was rude, but he——'

'Nathan behaved disgracefully,' Brenna contradicted firmly, sure that Carolyn would be blaming herself for Nathan's erroneous assumptions if she didn't stop her right now.

'He was just concerned——'

'He told me what he said to you and Nick while I was packing; he was very insulting.'

'Hey, you're lucky to have a brother to be that worried about you,' Carolyn scolded. 'The poor man walked in on a situation he didn't understand—and which you certainly hadn't explained to him, what was he supposed to think?'

'He could have waited for the explanations——'

'With me coming on to him like the vamp of the year?' her friend laughed. 'He probably thought I was trying to draw him into our happy circle.'

There had been no 'probably' about the assumption, that was exactly what Nathan had thought was happening. 'Stop defending him, Carolyn,' scolded Brenna.

'I'd defend any man who sent me white roses,' the other girl assured her. 'Still, if he isn't there, I'll have to thank him another time. Are you going to be in later today?' she changed the subject.

'You're coming back to town?' Brenna guessed with a groan, knowing they would never meet their deadline if Carolyn came back to London and joined her usual hectic social whirl.

'Don't sound so worried,' her friend laughed. 'I was a good girl after you left and stayed up all night finishing the story. So now Nick and I are going to reward ourselves by having a good time. I wondered if I could drop the rest of the story off to you when we get back. Although I don't suppose you feel much like working with Nathan there,' she realised.

'I'll be glad of an excuse to shut myself away from him for a few hours,' said Brenna darkly.

Carolyn chuckled softly. 'Is he going to be staying long?'

'Who knows?' Brenna dismissed drily. 'Nathan is a law unto himself.'

'I thought he was very sexy——'

'Carolyn!'

'Sorry, force of habit.' The grimace could be heard in her voice. 'Poor Nick will be getting a handful when he marries me!'

'He doesn't look as if he minds too much,' Brenna teased Nick's obvious adoration of his fiancée.

'No,' Carolyn laughed. 'And perhaps I'll get to meet your sister this afternoon.'

'Er—she won't be here,' Brenna excused quickly. 'She—she's visiting relatives,' she invented.

'Oh well, at least I'll get to see Nathan again.'

'Will you behave yourself!'

'When have you ever known me to do that?' her friend taunted.

'Never,' sighed Brenna. 'That's what I'm afraid of!'

'Don't be,' Carolyn laughed. 'Nathan can take care of himself.'

That was more than obvious. 'Actually, I was thinking of you——'

'Stop fussing, Brenna,' her friend advised impatiently. 'Nathan and I are both adults. I'll see you later,' she finished.

Brenna couldn't believe how late she had slept, although there was still time to catch her father at the office before he went to lunch, if she telephoned now. The Wade family might dismiss him as being unimportant, but he was Lesli's father, and he had a right to know what was happening with her at the moment.

'I was right about that T-shirt,' Nathan drawled behind her, startling her. 'It is more provocative than bare flesh,' he rasped.

Brenna had been so deep in thought she hadn't been aware of his entrance, and she followed his gaze down over the pointed allure of her breasts beneath the loose material to the tantalising length of her legs.

'You ought to have a public health warning slapped on you like cigarette packets do,' he growled. 'You *could* damage any man's health!'

Embarrassed colour darkened her cheeks. 'You shouldn't make remarks like that to me,' she snapped.

'No, I suppose not,' he sighed. 'I hope you don't mind, I borrowed your door key so I could let myself in again. Any calls while I was out?' His brows rose pointedly at the way she was still standing next to the telephone.

'Carolyn. To thank you for the roses,' she taunted. 'It was a thoughtful gesture, Nathan.'

'And totally unworthy of me,' he drawled. 'I owed her an apology and so I made it in the only way available to me.' He shrugged.

'Where have you been to this morning?' She saw his gaze move pointedly to the message he had left for her on the notepad. 'It only says out,' she defended.

'My times are all out, and when I got up at four this morning I crept around trying not to wake you. By eight o'clock I realised I could have saved myself the trouble; nothing was going to disturb you! So I took myself out for breakfast, and then went for a walk. I had no idea you had fallen into the habit of sleeping until lunchtime,' he said sarcastically.

'It must be the lax company I keep,' Brenna dismissed tartly. 'Now if you'll excuse me I have to get dressed and go out for a while. I shouldn't be long, just an hour or so.' While she had been talking to him the noon hour had passed, and her father always left the office where he worked promptly at twelve o'clock for his lunch. But she knew where he usually went, and would see him there.

'Boy-friend?' Nathan's eyes were narrowed.

'No!' she flashed.

'Can't you put off seeing your friends for a few days, until we have this mess with Lesli sorted out?' he rasped accusingly.

Her eyes were deeply green. 'I'm not seeing a friend either!'

'Who then?'

She met his gaze challengingly. 'I think a father has a right to know when his daughter has left her husband and just disappeared.'

'*Your* father?' Nathan realised harshly, his mouth a forbidding line.

'Of course,' she retorted.

'When did you start seeing him again?'

Brenna swung away from him as he would have reached for her. 'You make it sound as if I decided to stop,' she rasped. 'The Wades were the ones who prevented my seeing him from the time I was twelve years old. As soon as I got back to England four years ago I looked him up.'

'Why?'

'What do you mean, *why*?' she repeated incredulously. 'He didn't stop being my father just because the Wades decreed it!'

'Stop blaming us for every damn thing that's ever gone wrong in your life. We didn't make your father into the irresponsible drunk that he is.'

'Didn't you?' she scorned. 'It often happens when a man's family is taken from him.'

'Your father lost his family because he was too damned careless of it!'

They glared at each other across the width of the lounge, Nathan wearing the denims of the night before and a short-sleeved cotton shirt the same silver-grey of his eyes. Brenna knew that her own lack of clothing put her at a disadvantage, but she didn't particularly care about that at the moment.

'Your father made him what he is,' she bit out hardly.

'No one makes another person into a drunk!'

'"You can lead a horse to water but you can't make him drink"?' she quoted. 'No, but you can force the circumstances upon that person to push that first drink, and then another, down their throat,' she accused bitterly.

'Your father was always a drunk,' Nathan said disgustedly.

Her mouth twisted. 'I'm sure that's what you would like to think, but it isn't true.'

'Brenna——'

'I'm going out to see my father,' she met his gaze steadily. 'And nothing you say will stop me.'

'I wasn't trying to stop you seeing him,' he ran a hand through the thickness of his dark hair. 'You've just never mentioned that you were seeing your father again,' he frowned.

'Was I supposed to?' she challenged.

'Unless you felt the need to hide it,' he nodded slowly.

Her eyes flashed. 'He's my father, I'll see him when I want to. And I don't need anyone's permission!'

'I didn't say you did.'

'You implied it,' she snapped.

'Brenna, your father is a sick man,' he reasoned gently. 'Alcoholism is a disease——'

'All the more reason for his daughter to care what happens to him!'

He gave a deep sigh at her stubbornness. 'Can I come with you?' he asked softly.

She gave a scornful laugh. 'He hasn't touched a drink for almost a month, seeing me with a Wade is likely to put him right back at the bottom of a whisky bottle!' she understated.

'You know that the abstinence won't last, don't you?' Nathan said gently. 'That he can't stop drinking for any length of time?'

'Yes, I know,' she rasped. 'But while it lasts I give him all the encouragement I can.'

'That's commendable. But——'

'I have to go, Nathan,' she dismissed with controlled impatience. 'There's food in the fridge if you're hungry; I'll be eating out.'

He grabbed hold of her arm as she would have walked past him, his fingers lean and strong. 'When will you be back?' he ground out roughly.

'I told you, about an hour. And try not to upset Lesli if she should turn up here,' she sighed. 'Or she's likely to just leave again!'

His mouth tightened. 'Believe it or not, Lesli has always liked me.'

'She always did have poor taste—Nathan, no!' Brenna cried as he would have pulled her into his arms. 'Please don't touch me!'

He released her slowly, frowning darkly. 'You're as jumpy as a skittish——'

'Mare,' she finished drily, badly shaken by the physical threat this man posed. 'That is the rest of the crude terminology I heard you once discussing with one of the hands?'

Nathan grimaced, thrusting his hands into the pockets of his denims. 'I was a lot younger then, and you shouldn't have been listening,' he muttered.

'You were both standing just below my bedroom window at the time,' she drawled.

He scowled. 'You still shouldn't have been listening.'

She laughed derisively. 'Whatever happened to Kay McCrae?' she mocked. The other woman had been his girl-friend at the time he made the comment—and the woman he was also referring to.

'She's married and got three kids,' he mumbled reluctantly.

'Then I guess it must have been the stud that made her so jumpy,' Brenna taunted before fleeing the room, locking the bathroom door behind her as she heard him in hot pursuit.

She let her breath shakily from her body. She had tried so hard to keep Nathan at a brotherly distance, but he kept overstepping that imaginary line, and she knew that if she hadn't stopped him just now she would probably be in his arms even now.

He was sitting in the kitchen drinking coffee when she came back from her bedroom a few minutes later. 'Too many of those will give you a middle-aged spread,' she indicated the biscuit barrel he was liberally tucking into.

'I'll spread *you* across my knee and tan your backside if you don't get out of here!' he warned.

'I'd like to see you try,' she challenged, no longer wary of these physical retributions he kept threatening. 'It might have worked when I was seventeen, but I just might hit back at twenty-two!'

'Now *that* might be worth seeing——' Nathan began to rise threateningly.

Brenna left with as much haste as dignity would allow, knowing he had nerve enough to carry out the threat now that she had promised retribution.

She took a taxi to the restaurant her father frequented, never having bothered to acquire her own transport while living in London; tubes were plentiful, taxis even more so, and much more convenient than trying to fight her own way through the traffic.

Her father was seated at his usual table, and

she was relieved to see the glass of water he had
to accompany his meal; she was well aware that
he could relapse into drinking at any time, had
lived with the worry of what the alcohol was
doing to him for the last four years, since she had
really become aware of his problem. He just
didn't seem able to give it up for any length of
time. Much as it pained her to accept it she knew
it would one day kill him.

'Hello, love,' he stood up as she approached,
surprised to see her there, a tall loose-limbed man
who lived on his nerves. 'I thought you were in a
cottage somewhere in the middle of Wales?'

'Cumbria,' she corrected lightly, used to the
lapses of memory he occasionally had too, smiling
her thanks at the waiter as he brought her a menu.

'What happened, Brenna?' he asked astutely.

'Happened?' she delayed lightly. 'Lesli has had
a bit of an argument with Grant, but other than
that everything is going smoothly.'

His hazel eyes were narrowed. 'How serious is
a "bit of an argument"?'

'Nothing for you to worry about.' She had
thought better on the drive over here of worrying
him with Lesli's disappearance; he was doing so
well this time in his effort to keep away from
alcohol, she didn't want to give him reason to
start drinking again. Over the years she had kept
him informed about the happenings in both her
and Lesli's lives, but there was no point in
worrying him with this, she had decided.
'Pregnant women are notoriously temperamental,'
she dismissed lightly.

'I remember,' he drawled. 'But I always thought Lesli was the placid one of my daughters,' he frowned.

He wouldn't think that if he could see her sister during one of her sulks to get her own way! Lesli was placid only until she decided she wanted something to happen a certain way, then she changed completely.

'She is,' Brenna nodded. 'I'm sure all this will quickly pass. What have you ordered for lunch?' she changed the subject, ordering the same when she knew he had ordered the fresh fruit and cottage cheese.

It was just an hour later that she arrived back at the flat, moving quietly through the lounge when she saw Nathan was asleep stretched out on the sofa. Jet-lag was a terrible thing to go through, and she knew it didn't get any better, no matter how many times you flew.

Her studio was as she last saw it, the bed neatly made, her sketches lying about the work-tops. She worked on her latest drawing of Koly for the next hour and a half, and all remained quiet in the lounge as Nathan continued to sleep.

When the doorbell rang she hurried to answer it before it woke Nathan, and quietly invited Carolyn inside.

'I brought the . . . What is it?' Carolyn frowned as Brenna put a silencing finger up to her mouth.

'Nathan is asleep, and——'

'No, I'm not,' he appeared in the lounge doorway, his clothes rumpled, his hair tumbled, a sleepy look of sensuality in his eyes.

'Did I interrupt something?' Carolyn obviously misunderstood the reason for the latter.

'No.'

'Chance would be a fine thing,' Nathan grinned at Brenna's outraged expression, stretching like a sleek feline.

Carolyn turned to Brenna accusingly. 'And you said he was the one who never noticed you!'

Brenna mentally cringed at the mockery in Nathan's eyes before he drawled, 'Oh, I noticed her, but she can run faster than I can!'

'I wouldn't have thought a little thing like that would have bothered you,' Carolyn teased throatily, putting her arm through the crook of his as they went into the lounge together.

'Maybe Brenna already has a boy-friend?' He arched dark brows questioningly.

'I'm sure she doesn't,' Carolyn instantly shook her head. 'To tell you the truth, I think she's a little frightened of men.'

'Carolyn!' she protested at this assumption—a quite inaccurate one at that!

'She is?' Nathan ignored her outrage, looking at her with narrowed eyes.

'I think so,' her friend nodded. 'She hardly ever dates, and when she does, one date is all they get, poor things.'

'Really?' drawled Nathan, his gaze still riveted on the red-faced Brenna.

'Mm,' Carolyn frowned at her. 'I think she must have had a bad experience early on in life.'

'Carolyn, that's enough,' Brenna snapped irritably. 'I rarely date because I choose not to do so. Believe it or not, my life doesn't have to revolve around men!'

'Ouch!' Her friend gave a pained grimace. 'I think that dig was directed at me,' she assured Nathan lightly. 'We must have really upset her, Brenna never gets bitchy with me.'

'It wasn't directed at you at all,' Brenna blushed. 'It's men who seem to have the idea we can't do without them.'

'But we can't,' Carolyn drawled. 'And I for one don't even want to try!'

'A woman after my own heart,' Nathan grinned at her appreciatively.

Smiling buffoon! Brenna thought accusingly. Yesterday he couldn't even be bothered to give Carolyn the time of day, and now he was flirting with her as if he had never thought of her as anything but a beautifully desirable woman. And it was quite sickening the way Carolyn was fawning all over him as she thanked him for the roses, and equally nauseous was Nathan's charming flattery. The man was never charming, and he didn't know the meaning of the word flattery!

Finally Carolyn was the one who seemed to realise the two of them weren't alone, and she held out the folder she carried to Brenna. 'My second baby,' she drawled. 'Handle it with care,' she grimaced. 'Nick and I are off to New York for the weekend.'

'But it's only Thursday,' Brenna pointed out drily.

Her friend shrugged. 'Nick has some business

there, and I can't wait to get into the shops! Just send the story in to David when you've finished,' she dismissed carelessly. 'It was lovely seeing you again, Nathan.' She gave him a glowing smile. 'Maybe we can all have dinner together when Nick and I get back from New York?'

'I'm not sure I'll still be here then,' he evaded smoothly. 'Why don't you give Brenna a call when you get back to London; if I'm still here I'd love to join the three of you for dinner.'

'Oh, good,' Carolyn beamed. 'Now I really must go, Nick's waiting downstairs in the car.'

Her friend left in a waft of exclusive perfume, leaving an awkward silence behind her. Brenna was angry at both of them, and she wasn't sure whether it was for the way they had discussed her social life as if she weren't there or if it was the way they had flirted together as if she *definitely* weren't there!

'She must be difficult to keep up with,' Nathan murmured softly.

'Nick's used to it,' she snapped. 'In fact, I think he rather enjoys it. Before he met Carolyn he was very bored with his life; now he doesn't have the time to be bored,' she added ruefully.

'Nick Bancroft,' Nathan said the name slowly. 'His name somehow seems familiar to me. I— *Dominic* Bancroft?' he questioned incredulously.

Brenna gave an abrupt inclination of her head. 'Recent heir to all those oil millions,' she drawled. 'Wish you'd been more polite to him now, Nathan?' she taunted.

His mouth tightened. 'I'm not a snob, Brenna,' he rasped.

'Nick used to be,' she grimaced. 'He used to be so wrapped up in himself, very conceited and supercilious. But Carolyn has changed all that. She keeps him so much on his toes keeping up with her he doesn't have the time to think of himself!'

'I can imagine,' said Nathan. 'I didn't think she could live the way she does on what she earns as a writer.'

Her eyes flashed. 'Well, you're wrong, she does! She isn't interested in Nick's money, if that's what you think,' she snapped. 'Carolyn doesn't like jewellery, and she abhors furs, her only weakness is that she likes to travel. And she can afford to pay for that!'

'Believe it or not,' he drawled hardly, 'I like the lady. I wasn't being critical just now.'

'It just sounded that way,' she retorted harshly.

'Only if you're biased,' he grated. 'Why don't you date, Brenna?'

She stiffened at the unexpectedness of the question; she had thought he had let Carolyn's comments about her social life pass by. She should have known better! 'I date,' she told him calmly. 'When I choose to.'

'But nothing serious?' he persisted.

'As Carolyn said, I had a nasty experience early on in life,' she looked at him pointedly.

His eyes narrowed to icy slits. 'There was nothing nasty about that night. In fact, I've wanted to repeat it ever since,' he added softly.

Brenna's expression froze. 'I'm sure there've been plenty of other women to fill your bed since then!'

'A few,' he conceded drily. 'But that doesn't mean they have,' he added harshly at the contemptuous curve of her lips.

'My friends used to find you a fascinating topic of conversation, Nathan,' she dismissed. 'I think they worked it out that the longest you'd gone without a woman was two months; and that was only because you'd broken your leg skiing!'

'Six weeks,' he ground out. 'One of the nurses was very obliging.'

'Even more reason for me to know you haven't been alone the last sixteen months.'

'Didn't Lesli tell you?' he scorned. 'As I recall, you used to tell each other everything.'

'I made it clear I wasn't interested in knowing!'

Nathan released his breath in a ragged sigh. 'Maybe we should start this conversation all over again?' he muttered. 'How was your father?'

'You don't really want to know,' she said crossly.

'I am interested, damn you,' he said intently.

'Do the Wades need the satisfaction of knowing how their victim fared after a savaging from them?'

'Brenna, you're under a misapprehension concerning our involvement with your father's——'

'I don't think so,' she rasped, turning away. 'And he's well, very well.'

She wasn't aware how vulnerable the taut set of her shoulders was at that moment, but the man watching her was, and he reached for her instinctively.

'No!' He held her firm as she would have escaped him, turning her to press her face against his chest, his thumb lightly caressing her cheek as it rested against her. 'I need this,' he groaned into her hair. 'I think we both do!'

'Nathan, don't!' choked Brenna just before the firmness of his mouth moved softly over hers and the protests melted away as her body responded to a demand of its own too long denied.

Drugging kisses, ever deeper and deeper, put her mind awash, as the force of Nathan's desire pressed against the flatness of her stomach, the softness of her breasts flattened against his chest as his hands cupped her face and he drank from her mouth, sipping, thirsting, taking his fill.

A doorbell can be a shrill intruder to lovers long denied each other, and Brenna murmured protestingly at its insistent ringing, nuzzling demandingly against Nathan's mouth.

Finally he raised his eyes. 'Are you expecting anyone?'

'No one. Except—Lesli!' she realised desperately, pulling out of Nathan's arms to run and open the door.

Lesli, poor unhappy, very pregnant Lesli, threw herself into Brenna's arms. 'I can't go back there,' she sobbed. 'I *can't*!'

Brenna let her cry in her arms, too relieved to at last have her sister here to notice when Nathan appeared in the doorway behind them. Lesli's natural beauty had begun to glow during her pregnancy, her shoulder-length black hair was thick and shining, the hazel of her eyes clear and glowing with health, and she did not seem to have put on any weight other than the gentle swell that was her baby. But the ravages of the last few days showed in the unhappy droop to her mouth, her pale cheeks and the shadows in the depths of her eyes.

Finally Lesli was the one to see Nathan as he watched them with narrowed eyes. 'Nathan———!' she gasped accusingly, stepping back from Brenna, looking poised for flight. 'What's he doing here?' she demanded.

Brenna felt a sharp stab of pain at her sister's mistrust. So much for Nathan's claim that Lesli liked him; she looked as if she wanted to run from both of them at the moment!

'That's a silly question,' Nathan scolded firmly, moving to take Lesli's arm and direct her away from the open doorway and through to the lounge. 'We've all been concerned about you,' he reproved once he had sat her down on the sofa.

'Even Grant?' she said harshly, her eyes rebellious, her mouth quivering emotionally.

'Especially Grant,' he told her firmly.

'I suppose that's why you're here and he isn't?' she said bitterly.

Nathan glanced at Brenna for help, their own conflicts forgotten, even that lightning passion they had shared in each other's arms minutes ago, in the need to reassure Lesli that they all loved her and wanted to help her.

Brenna moved down on to her knees in front of her sister, taking her chilled hands into her own.

'I've spoken to Grant, Lesli,' she told her softly. 'He's very worried.'

'About me or his child?' Lesli rasped.

Brenna looked up at Nathan as she heard his sharp intake of breath, guessing the reason his eyes glazed over coldly as he returned her gaze; Lesli had almost repeated word for word her own scorned comment of yesterday! Surely he couldn't really think she ... Who gave a damn what he thought, she dismissed hardly; Lesli was the important one.

'Lesli, you know Grant loves you.'

'No,' Lesli cut in coldly. 'I *thought* he loved me. I was wrong.'

'Lesli, whatever he's done——'

'I don't want to talk about it,' Lesli answered Nathan in a hard voice.

'Darling, you have to——'

'No,' Lesli shook her head dully. 'I don't even want to think about it.'

Brenna turned helplessly to Nathan; she had never seen her sister like this before, so uncaring, so hardened. She didn't know how to deal with it.

'Lesli, I'm going to telephone Grant now,' Nathan told her briskly.

She stiffened. 'I don't want to speak to him,' she quivered.

'No one is asking you to do that,' he rasped. 'But since he's your husband I think he at least deserves to be told that you're safe. No one even knows where you've been the last four days.'

'I went to Oxford. I ... we used to live there, when we were children,' Lesli revealed abruptly.

It hadn't even occurred to Brenna that her sister would go there, and she gave Nathan a look of apology for not thinking of it. Lesli had always liked Oxfordshire; she should have realised she might go there.

'We have to call Grant now,' she squeezed Lesli's hand reassuringly. 'But you don't have to talk to him if you don't want to.'

'I don't,' Lesli shook her head in jerky movements.

Brenna shrugged in Nathan's direction as he made the call, concern for her sister etched into her face as she watched her anxiously. Whatever had gone wrong between Lesli and Grant was much more serious than she had thought, and she half believed the claim she had made to her father about pregnant women being over-emotional. Lesli was calm—too calm.

She could hear Nathan's half of the conversation with his brother, guessed that Grant wanted to talk to Lesli from the glances Nathan kept shooting their way as he refused the request. For all the notice Lesli took of the exchange it might not have been taking place.

Nathan put his hand over the mouthpiece as Grant must have insisted he speak with his wife. 'Lesli?' he frowned.

She shook her head firmly, her mouth set mutinously as she didn't even glance at him.

'He says if you won't come back to Canada, he's coming here,' Nathan told her softly.

Panic filled Lesli's eyes. 'I don't want him here!'

'That doesn't seem to be bothering him at the moment,' Nathan drawled.

'No,' she acknowledged bitterly. 'Brenna?' she questioned sharply.

Compassion softened Brenna's eyes, and she felt far older than her sister at that moment than two years younger. 'I think you should go back,' she encouraged softly.

Lesli's fingers clutched painfully at her hands. 'Only if you'll come with me!'

'Oh, but——'

'Brenna!' Nathan rasped warningly.

He didn't know what he was asking, neither of them did. But Lesli needed her, and her own feelings about returning to Canada had to come far second to that. She wordlessly nodded her head in agreement, wishing she hadn't seen that blaze of triumph in Nathan's eyes before he turned away to assure Grant that the three of them would be returning to Canada.

CHAPTER FOUR

CALGARY looked like most of the other western Canadian cities, as if it had been built with the sweat and hard labour of many men, a long sprawling city in the foothills of Alberta, with skyscrapers surrounding the tower in the centre of the city that owed most of its wealth and prosperity to the oil that had been found in the province, and reaching out in pretty housing complexes towards the distant Rockies themselves. It was a city that always seemed alive and humming. The usual local garb of denims and casual shirts, often worn with the customary slouched hat, for men, gave a deceptive impression of naïveté. The people of Calgary and its surrounding small towns just liked it that way.

The Wade ranch was about fifteen miles from town, the house itself being built on top of the hill, comprised mainly of windows, so that whatever way you looked you were confronted by the towering Rockies and Calgary itself.

Cattle grazed as far as the eye could see, a dozen or so horses exercising in a field neighbouring the house. It all looked very much as it had a year ago, and yet Brenna could feel her tension rising as Nathan stopped the Camaro in front of the house, having advised Grant to wait at the ranch before confronting Lesli. Which was perhaps as well, as her sister was tired and irritable and would probably have caused a scene if Grant had been waiting in the airport when they got through Customs.

Nathan came round to the front of the car to help Lesli out of the low vehicle, pushing the seat forward so that Brenna could climb out of the back. The sky was a still calm blue in early evening, the air crisp and warm, and she breathed it in deeply before they all entered the house to confront Grant.

He came out into the reception area to meet them. Lesli took one look at him, burst into tears, and ran down the hallway of the bungalow house to her bedroom, the door closing firmly.

'That was a good start,' Grant said shakily. The last few days had been a strain on him too, by the look of the tautness of the skin across his high cheekbones, his eyes dull with pain. 'Should I go to her, do you think?' He looked uncertainly at Brenna.

It was testimony to how much Lesli's leaving had shaken him that he should voice such a question; ordinarily he had as much self-assurance and arrogance as Nathan. 'Maybe not just yet,' Brenna advised gently; Lesli hadn't told her what had happened to make her leave her husband of four years, not during the long night hours when they had shared her bed, nor during the long flight back here, and she didn't believe Lesli was ready to talk to Grant just yet either. 'I'll take her some dinner on a tray, and then maybe tomorrow . . .'

'Yeah, maybe tomorrow.' Grant turned away defeatedly, and the study door closed behind him.

'Nathan?' Brenna turned to him in confusion, her expression pained.

His mouth twisted into the semblance of a smile. 'Not much of a homecoming for you.'

She knew what he meant, and he wasn't being his usual sarcastic self. In the past there had been arguments and disputes, usually with her in the thick of them, but it had never been like this; the family, what was left of it, was falling apart.

'We'll survive,' she said softly. 'I—Mindy!' she greeted warmly as the housekeeper came into the hallway. 'It's lovely to see you again.'

'Brenna.' The elderly woman stiffly accepted her hug. 'Your old room has been prepared—unless you would prefer a different one?'

'No—no, that will be fine.' Brenna frowned at the other woman's hardness. Because of Christine Wade's long and finally fatal illness, Mindy Fletcher had taken the two Wade boys under her wing and become like a second mother to them, and when Lesli and Brenna had arrived looking like a couple of confused birds who had fallen out of their nest, she had extended that same warmth to them; that warmth was no longer there, Mindy treating her like a guest rather than part of the family. It really *wasn't* much of a homecoming!

'Dinner will be ready in a few minutes, if you would like to wash up,' Mindy instructed.

'I thought I'd take a tray to Lesli.'

'I can do that,' Mindy told her abruptly. 'There's no need to trouble yourself.'

'Oh, but——'

'Unless you don't think Lesli would like to see me?' The elderly woman arched greying brows. Her dark curly hair had a similar peppered effect, and her weathered face was kind, but stern. And if she ever wore anything else but trousers and a blouse beneath a blue or brown smock Brenna had never seen it.

'I'm sure she would,' she assured the housekeeper gently. 'I just——'

Mindy turned away to return to the kitchen, where she could be heard muttering something about 'flighty young girls who didn't know when they had it good'!

Nathan grinned at Brenna as she turned to look at him with questioning eyes. 'Mindy has never forgiven you for not coming home to live last year,' he drawled, starting to walk up the stairs with her cases to the attic room that had always been Brenna's, while Brenna trailed halfheartedly behind him. 'And I'm afraid Lesli leaving Grant has put the Jordan women right out of favour!' he added drily.

'I gathered,' she grimaced, following him into the room at the top of the stairs. The windows extended to the sloping roof in this one room. She had always loved to draw, and before she arrived ten years ago Patrick Wade had ordered that this room be made into a bedroom-studio for her. Everything looked the same as it always had, the pretty rose and cream of the decor not in the least detracted from by the easels and workbenches in the other section of the room.

She had a little difficulty looking at the bed, considering what had happened the last time she had lain beneath the pink lace canopy. But Nathan didn't seem to be bothered by the same memory as he stacked her cases on the ottoman at the foot of her bed, so Brenna forced them from her mind too.

'I have a few phone calls to make before dinner,' he told her tersely. 'But as Mindy is on the warpath I wouldn't be late down.'

'No,' she sighed. 'I think I'll just freshen up and then go and see Lesli anyway; she might feel like talking now she's back home.'

Nathan's mouth twisted. 'That wasn't the impression I got.'

'Nor me,' she frowned. 'I'm sure all this can't be good for the baby.'

'I'll see about getting her an appointment to see the doctor as soon as possible,' he nodded grimly. 'She didn't look too well to me on the flight over.'

She hadn't to Brenna either, seeming to sleep too much for her sister's peace of mind. And if Lesli's mad flight to England had harmed the baby in any way, Brenna knew her sister would never forgive herself; she badly wanted the baby she had waited so long to conceive.

'Don't look so worried.' Nathan gently touched her cheek with a calloused hand. 'I'm sure everything is going to work out.'

It was evidence of how weary she was herself that Brenna pressed weakly against that hand, offering no resistance when Nathan put a hand beneath her chin to lift her face up to his and claim her mouth with his own.

Like a moth to a flame, she thought bitterly, as her mouth tingled from the caress and her body caught fire. Nathan growled low in his throat at her lack of resistance, his arms about her like steel bands as he moulded her body into his.

'I've brought you up a tray of coffee.' Mindy banged the tray down on the dressing-table, and Brenna and Nathan instantly pulled apart.

Brenna turned to the older woman with burning cheeks. 'Thank you. I . . . Please don't misunderstand——'

'It's none of my business if Nathan chooses to make a fool of himself,' Mindy snapped disapprovingly. 'Again,' she added disgustedly, before closing the door behind her with a firm thud.

Brenna frowned her embarrassed confusion. That she had allowed the kiss to happen was bad enough, but that Mindy should witness it somehow made it worse, her harshly spoken comments barbed if not understood.

'She's better than a cold shower,' Nathan said ruefully. 'Much more effective.'

'Nathan——'

'I know,' he sighed. 'The kiss should never have happened. You don't know why it did. Let's forget the whole thing,' he added derisively.

'Yes,' she agreed simply.

'It's already forgotten,' he dismissed hardly, striding to the door. 'Drink your coffee before it gets cold,' he instructed coldly.

It was easy, much too easy, to say the kiss should never have happened, and to forget it! It had happened, and after all her certainty that she had despised Nathan. She *did* despise him, but the desire she had feared, in herself and in him, was still there. And it could rage out of control at any time.

But this time she couldn't run away from it; she had to think of Lesli and the baby. She had told her father she was going to Canada to spend a few weeks with Lesli before the baby was born, and because of the fraught situation between Grant and Lesli she knew she had no choice but to go through with that. She would just have to make the best of the situation and ignore Nathan when she could. Which was virtually impossible.

She showered and changed while she drank down several cups of the coffee—the Wades had never been a family to dress for dinner, and her black trousers and dark green blouse were casually comfortable, her height added to by high-heeled sandals, her hair secured in a loose knot on top of her head; it was cooler that way.

Lesli lay back against the pillows of the double bed when Brenna entered the room a few minutes later. The half of the bed that Grant usually occupied was smooth and unruffled. The dinner tray lay untouched on the bedside table, the food growing cold.

'Lesli . . .'

'I should never have allowed myself to be talked into coming back here,' Lesli suddenly choked, tears streaming down her face. 'Now I'll never get away!'

Brenna sat down on the bed beside her. 'This isn't a prison, Lesli.'

'Isn't it?' her sister retorted in a hard voice. 'How can you say that when you couldn't wait to leave?'

'But you're married to Grant.'

'And you should have been married to Nathan,' her sister claimed.

Brenna swallowed hard. 'What do you mean?'

'Grant and I knew you'd spent the night with Nathan before you left last year,' Lesli explained huskily. 'Grant challenged Nathan about it, and he said the two of you were going to be married.'

Brenna shook her head dazedly. 'You've never mentioned that you knew before.'

'Nathan asked us not to, because you would have been embarrassed, I suppose. But don't you see, Brenna?' she reasoned desperately. 'You more than anyone must be able to understand why I want a divorce.'

'A divorce!' Brenna repeated astoundedly, standing up. 'Lesli?'

'Grant doesn't love me,' her sister stated flatly.

'But do you love him?' she probed gently.

Lesli's mouth tightened even more. 'Not any more.'

She actually sounded as if she meant it, Brenna realised. How could a love as deep as the one Lesli had always had for Grant die so suddenly—and so completely?

'Lesli, you're carrying his child!'

'*My* child,' her sister contradicted. 'It's in my body, so it belongs to me.'

'But it's part of Grant,' Brenna reason.

'I'll try and forget that.' Lesli sank down under the bedclothes. 'Could you take this tray away; I'd like to get some sleep now.'

'You haven't eaten anything,' said Brenna worriedly.

'I don't want it.'

'Lesli——' Brenna broke off as her sister turned the other way, biting her bottom lip as her sister's pain became her own.

'Brenna,' Lesli stopped her at the door. 'Make sure Grant realises he isn't welcome in this room any more,' she rasped.

Brenna sighed. 'Don't you think you should be the one to tell him that?'

'No,' her sister muttered. 'I don't even want to see him.'

'Darling, you can't stay in here for ever, and——'

'I don't want to see him!'

With a last worried look at her sister's averted face Brenna quietly left the room. How did you tell a man he wasn't welcome in the bed he had shared with Lesli for the last four years?

'Don't worry,' Grant told her harshly as Brenna haltingly tried to tell him that, minutes later in the study where he sat behind the desk in the swivel oak chair that was rather like the old-fashioned type the sheriff always had in cowboy films. 'I haven't been able to sleep in that bed since she left, and it seems even more unwelcoming now that she's back!'

Brenna's fingers were laced together in her lap.

'Grant, Lesli seems to have the idea that you no longer love her, and——'

'That's a damned lie,' he grated. 'Of course I love her!'

She moistened her lips. 'If you've had an affair——'

'Is that what Lesli said I've done?' he attacked fiercely. 'My God, I don't even look at other women, let alone go to bed with them!' He stood up forcefully.

'Calm down, Grant,' she sighed wearily. An affair was obviously *not* the reason for their conflict. 'Lesli hasn't told me anything. Neither of you has, that's why I'm stumbling around in the dark trying to make sense of this!'

His expression became defensive. 'This isn't really any of your business, is it? You and Nathan both keep sticking your nose in, and it's nothing to do with either of you. Lesli and I will work this out on our own.'

'How?' she questioned tautly. 'Lesli won't even agree to talk to you, and you seem just as stubborn!'

'That doesn't mean we need you and Nathan——'

'What about the baby?' Brenna cut in coldly. 'Where does that fit into all this?'

'It's our baby and——'

'Lesli says it's hers,' she sighed. 'And when she divorces you——'

'Divorce!' All the colour left his face as he stood up noisily. 'She isn't divorcing me!'

'She says she is,' Brenna frowned.

'Like hell she is!' Grant grated harshly. 'I'll divorce her first!'

It occurred to Brenna at that moment that Grant wasn't talking very logically; it also occurred to her that it might have something to do with the half empty bottle of whisky beside him on the desk. Grant was drunk! She had never seen any of the Wade men drink more than a couple of glasses of wine with their meal, and a few bottles of alcohol were usually only kept in the house for guests. Any guest wanting whisky in the near future was going to be out of luck!

Brenna stood up. 'Maybe we'd better talk when you're—feeling better——'

'Not drunk, you mean.' Grant slumped back into the chair, putting his feet up on the desk. 'There will be no divorce, Brenna, not now or ever,' he spoke with finality. 'Lesli will come to her senses eventually.'

She wasn't so sure of that, and a frown marred her brow as she waited in the lounge for Nathan to finish his calls and come down for dinner; Mindy had already been in twice, given a disgusted snort that her dinner was being kept waiting, and left again.

Nathan looked unperturbed when he joined Brenna a short time later, having changed into fitted beige trousers and a brown and beige striped shirt. 'Has Mindy got to the slamming door stage yet?' he grimaced.

'Not yet. But——'

'Oh, we're all right, then,' he said confidently, pulling out the chair opposite his that had always been Brenna's place at the dining-table and pressing the buzzer for Mindy to begin serving their meal. 'I know, I'm dicing with death,' he shrugged as Brenna pulled a face. 'Better attack than defence.'

He grinned up at Mindy as she served their meal, and before the elderly woman left to get their main course he had even managed to coax a smile out of her.

'You always were her favourite,' Brenna said disgustedly.

'I was always the one who had to find ways of getting back into her good graces,' he corrected. 'It was either learn how to charm her or spend half my life in my bedroom.'

Charm. Yes, for a man who never used it he certainly knew how to get around Mindy. The housekeeper was actually laughing by the time she served them coffee in the lounge.

'Right,' Nathan sobered once he and Brenna were alone. 'What's happening between Lesli and Grant?'

'Nothing,' Brenna sighed. 'She's pretending to sleep—or she just might not be pretending; she seemed very tired. And Grant is drunk——'

'Out cold,' Nathan corrected gruffly. 'I put him to bed in one of the guest rooms.'

'That's why you were so late down?' Brenna frowned.

He nodded. 'There'd be hell to pay if Mindy had found him.'

Brenna stood up to pace the room. 'I don't understand what's wrong with them. Lesli says

Grant doesn't love her, but I'm sure he does. She—she seems hard—*hardened*. It's hard to describe.'

'I've seen it for myself. It's as if she's willing herself not to love him,' he frowned.

'He says he hasn't had an affair.'

'I know damn well he hasn't,' Nathan rasped, his eyes narrowed. 'And if Lesli says otherwise——'

'She doesn't,' she shook her head. 'Nathan, we have to do something or—or I'm afraid it will be too late.'

'Meaning?' he prompted harshly, his expression hardening as she told him about both Grant and Lesli mentioning divorce. 'Young idiots!' he grated. 'Don't they realise that once that word gets taken seriously everything else gets distorted?'

'I don't think they care,' Brenna sighed. 'Not at the moment, anyway.'

'Then we'll have to make sure they're given time to care,' he scowled.

It was strange how the two of them were working together, even becoming friends in their common cause to save Grant and Lesli's marriage. It was so long since she had felt even half this close to Nathan; she had forgotten how good it felt.

He glanced at his watch. 'Grant is going to be out until the morning. Lesli will probably be asleep until then, so I have a little time to work something out. I have to go, I have an appointment in the city.'

'Now?' she frowned her surprise.

'Half an hour ago, actually, but never mind. You probably feel like an early night yourself. I'll give all this some thought while I'm out.' He stood up.

He was gone so fast Brenna was just left with a blur of expensive aftershave, and she was slowly drinking her coffee when Mindy came in to clear away.

'Has Nathan gone out?' The older woman frowned at his absence.

'He said he had an appointment in town,' Brenna explained with a smile.

'I should have known,' Mindy said indulgently. 'I expect he's gone to see Dee.'

'Dee?' Brenna repeated with a feigned lack of interest.

'Dee Wallace,' the housekeeper explained. 'She owns a boutique in the city. The two of them have been seeing each other for several months now.'

The fact that Mindy took such care to tell her that made her wonder if the other woman could also know of the night she had spent with Nathan last year. It was a possibility, she acknowledged. Mindy was the housekeeper, and she seemed to know most of what went on in the household. But Mindy needn't have worried about warning her off Nathan; the two of them might be trying to keep Lesli and Grant together, but she wasn't silly enough to see anything else between them. She hadn't been even that naïve a first time, let alone a second!

CHAPTER FIVE

'COME on, sleepyhead,' a deep voice tormented. 'No one stays in bed after six o'clock here!'

Brenna gave a groan, clutching the sheet to her breasts as she rolled over to blink up at Nathan. 'I've always hated the way you're so disgustingly cheerful this time of morning,' she scowled, smoothing back the tangle of her hair. 'It's indecent!' Especially considering she knew he hadn't returned to the ranch by the time she had fallen asleep five hours ago! Maybe he had just returned?

His hair was still damp from taking a shower, his checked shirt partly unbuttoned, his denims even more faded and snug-fitting than the ones he had worn in London. If anything was indecent this morning it was the sensuality he *oozed*!

'What do you want?' she asked crossly, fixing him with a glowering glare as he snorted scornfully at the provocation of that remark. 'And no crude remarks, thank you,' she snapped. 'I'm not in the mood for them.'

Nathan's eyes crinkled at the corners as he smiled at her, and Brenna was struck by the realisation that he had smiled more in the last few days than she had seen for a long time. 'The sun's up, the horses are saddled,' he drawled. 'And I thought you might like to escape the tension in the house for an hour or so.'

'How are they both this morning?' she frowned.

'Lesli is still sleeping, and Grant is walking around as if the sound of an eggshell breaking would be like a rocket going off inside his head,' he revealed ruefully. 'I think it's best to stay away from him for at least a couple of hours.'

'And how is your head?' Brenna arched black brows.

'Mine?' he frowned. 'You know I rarely touch the stuff.'

She avoided his eyes. 'Mindy said you were out with—a friend, yesterday evening,' she revealed huskily. 'You can't have had much sleep.'

'Enough,' he rasped tautly. 'And Mindy talks too damned much.' His eyes were darkened with displeasure.

'I think she was warning me off,' her derisive tone mocked the necessity of that. 'Everyone in the household seems to know about that night we spent together,' she added awkwardly, not sure what his reaction was going to be to its being such public knowledge.

'Then they must also have realised it was a mistake,' he said harshly. 'Now are you coming for that ride or not?' His eyes were steely slits.

'I am,' she nodded abruptly. 'I'll meet you downstairs in ten minutes.'

'Don't worry,' he said jeeringly. 'I didn't intend waiting here for you.'

He made her feel about ten years old! Probably

Dee Wallace was one of the sophisticated women he usually dated, a woman who enjoyed a physical relationship with him without hesitation or embarrassment, who thought nothing of sharing the intimacy of nakedness with him. He had succeeded in making her feel gauche and immature.

But she forgot all that once she was up on Samson's back. He was a beautiful pure black gelding, a gift from her mother and Patrick on her sixteenth birthday. The gentle giant, she had dubbed him the first time she rode him, and so he had become Samson. He had whinnied in recognition as soon as she walked into the stable, seeming pleased to have her up on his back after such a long absence.

'I've been keeping him exercised for you.' Nathan steadied his stallion down to a walk beside Samson as they left the stables, although his beautiful chestnut animal obviously wanted to gallop off across the meadows. 'I knew you would be back.'

Brenna glanced up at him sharply. 'I'm only here for as long as Lesli needs me.'

'If that were true you would never have left in the first place!'

'What are you talking about?' she frowned.

'Do you have any idea what a blow it was to Lesli when you decided to stay on in London instead of coming back here?' he grated.

'I had to break away some time,' she snapped, for once the beauty of the herd of prize Herefords, with their beautiful short red and white coats, lost on her. Patrick had spent years perfecting his herd of beef cattle, and though Brenna abhorred their fate she had to admit they were truly beautiful animals.

'If you had married and gone away I think Lesli could have accepted it,' rasped Nathan. 'But just not coming home . . .'

She flushed at his accusation. 'I had my own life to live. I've never liked what this ranch stood for, you know that.' She hoped her lack of conviction wasn't as apparent to him as it was to her. She did hate ranching cattle for beef, but just being back here in the foothills of Calgary, with the Rockies in the distance, the air so clean and fresh, made her wonder why she had thought she didn't belong here. She belonged here just as much as she did in England!

'Back to that again,' Nathan sighed. 'We were talking about the way you let Lesli down.'

'I didn't,' she claimed indignantly. 'I had to leave the family some time; it seemed like the right time.'

'You and Lesli were always so much closer than just sisters.' His hat was pulled low, his eyes narrowed against the bright sun.

'She has Grant now,' Brenna told him firmly. 'At least, she did.' Her face clouded.

'She still does,' he grated.

'What are we going to do about them, Nathan?' she appealed.

'As long as we can keep them both here we have nothing to worry about. I telephoned Lesli's doctor this morning, and he——'

'This morning?' she echoed in surprise.

'He's a friend,' Nathan said in amusement.

'He would need to be,' she grimaced; it was only six-thirty now!

'We were at college together,' he drawled. 'He's going to see her this morning, and I'm hoping I can persuade him to take her into hospital for a few days. Don't look so worried,' he hastened to assure her as she paled. 'I'm sure nothing is wrong, but a few days' rest wouldn't hurt her, and it would give her breathing space without being as drastic as running away again or asking Grant for a divorce.'

'You had time to think of this last night?' she queried cynically, enjoying the gentle breeze that ruffled the tendrils of hair at her nape that had escaped being pushed beneath her cream hat.

Nathan gave her an icy look. 'I don't know what Mindy told you——'

'Enough,' she taunted.

'It sounds like too damned much to me,' he glared. 'She may have been with the family thirty years——'

'She's *part* of the family, Nathan,' Brenna laughed. 'And you'll never shut her up. If you tried to stop her she'd just look at you with hurt in her eyes and you'd feel awful.'

He sighed. 'You're probably right,' he agreed. 'But Dee is only a friend, and I don't like Mindy speculating that there's more to it than that.'

Mindy wasn't the type to speculate, and they both knew it. Brenna knew she should have felt relieved that Nathan had a steady girl-friend he was serious about, and yet it was hard to imagine Nathan bringing another woman to the ranch as his wife. But he would eventually marry, he was too sensual a man to go through life alone, and he had become bored with the challenge of a lot of different relationships years ago. And at thirty-six she doubted he would wait much longer before marrying. Maybe it was dog-in-manger of her considering she didn't want him for herself, but she truly couldn't imagine any other woman as his wife.

'Do you think your doctor friend will go for admitting Lesli?' she changed the subject.

'I think so,' he nodded. 'Just for a rest.'

'And is Lesli going to accept it, do you think?' she asked with a grimace for her sister's co-operation.

'I get the impression she'd do anything to get out of the house and away from Grant,' he scowled.

'Yes,' she sighed.

'Did you do much riding in England?' he challenged suddenly, reining in the stallion as he became even more anxious for a gallop.

'Not much,' she admitted.

'Want to race me back to the ranch?'

Brenna swung around in the saddle, surprised to see they had come a good couple of miles from the house. 'I'm a little rusty,' she protested, her body already complaining at the unaccustomed exercise.

'Riding a horse is like making love——'

'Once you've done it once you never forget,' she finished hardly.

His face darkened with irritation at her accusing tone. 'Brenna . . .'

'Let's go, shall we, Nathan?' She turned Samson and set him at a gallop, her hat falling down on to her back, her hair streaming out wildly behind her, much silkier and finer than Samson's tail, but making her look one with the blue-black animal.

She wasn't at all surprised when Nathan and the stallion streaked past her a good mile from home, and she urged Samson to greater speed, although she knew he would never catch the other pair.

She jumped nimbly down from Samson's back once in the stable yard and handed the reins to Bill, her cheeks flushed, her eyes sparkling, her hair a tangle of ebony waves down her spine.

She gave a start of surprise as strong sinewed arms came about her waist from behind and she felt Nathan's warm breath against her ear as he moulded his body into the back of hers.

'You're completely wild and untamed,' he groaned.

'Nathan . . .'

'No.' He stilled her struggles. 'You can't keep escaping me.'

'But I don't want this!' She couldn't get his arms from about her, like steel bands against her pulling fingers, their voices necessarily hushed because Bill was settling the two horses back into their stalls.

Suddenly Nathan thrust her away from him, his eyes flinty, and just as cutting. 'What did you want from me that night?' he rasped. 'Just to find out what it would be like with me after all that talk with your friends? To rid yourself of your cumbersome virginity with an experienced older man? What?' he demanded. 'Because it sure as hell wasn't a proposal you were expecting!'

Brenna still had no real explanation for what had happened that night for herself, let alone for him. She hadn't had so much to drink she didn't know exactly what she was doing, and who she was doing it with. At the time she had just wanted to be in his arms, to seek oblivion, and if there had been more to it than that she had never probed it.

'Of course I didn't expect it,' she snapped. 'You'd never given any indication before that you felt that way about me.'

Nathan's hands clenched into fists at his sides. 'That way?' he mocked. 'Why can't you say it—I loved you! I certainly don't go around proposing marriage to every woman I've slept with,' he rasped.

'I don't think the house could hold that many wives!' Her eyes flashed like emeralds.

He drew in a ragged breath. 'I don't understand you, I doubt if I ever will. When a man offers you his love and his life it's usually polite to at least tell him you don't want them!'

'Nathan, you . . .' Brenna became conscious of their stunned audience, her face blanching at the shocked look on Bill's face. He had been employed on the Wade ranch ever since she had lived here, had been a witness to many of the fiery arguments between Nathan and herself, but never one quite as bitterly personal as this one. She turned accusing eyes on Nathan. 'I'm here because my sister's marriage is in trouble,' she grated. 'But once that's settled again I'm leaving here on the next plane and I never want to see you again!'

'Even that might be too soon for me!' He turned and strode out of the stable, knocking the dust from his hat against his thigh as he walked.

'Patrick always said the two of you could light a fire during one of your arguments,' Bill whistled between his teeth. 'I think I've got the blisters to prove it!'

Some of the tension left Brenna's body—but not all. She doubted she would be able to completely relax again until she left here and returned to England. Maybe that was why she had felt that instant rapport with England four years ago; there was no Nathan there to mock and taunt and deride everything she did.

'You only caught the edge of it, Bill,' she grimaced. 'I have third-degree burns!'

He chuckled, a middle-aged ranch hand who loved his work. 'It's good to have you back, Brenna,' he said with obvious sincerity. 'It just hasn't been the same around here without you.'

'All that peace and quiet getting to you, was it, Bill?' she teased.

He nodded. 'It's been a long time since I've seen Nathan blow up like that.'

'You wouldn't have enjoyed it so much if you'd been on the receiving end of it!'

'Now that you're back I expect I will be—I expect we *all* will be,' he grinned. 'It's been pretty dull around here the last year or so.'

As she and Nathan had argued more or less from the moment they had met Brenna couldn't understand why Bill preferred it that way. 'I think I'll go and get some coffee,' she murmured. 'Nice to see you again, Bill.' She didn't need to have the remark returned, she could see how much he was enjoying himself by the twinkle in his blue eyes.

When she would prefer the tanquillity of her life without Nathan in it she found it strange to think other people actually welcomed the combustion between them. Maybe Bill was just a glutton for punishment!

Or maybe it wasn't just Bill who had these masochistic tendencies; Grant seemed to be spoiling for a fight as she entered the house, his voice raised at his older brother.

'—and I tell you she's *my* wife, so I'll take her to the damned doctor!' He glared at Nathan in mulish determination.

If Brenna had thought he looked in bad shape the night before, he looked even worse now; his handsome face was deathly pale, his blue eyes sunken into the dark shadows of their sockets, his fair hair looking in need of a comb. Physically he and Nathan looked very alike, both tall and muscular, but Grant had his mother's fair colouring whereas Nathan took after his father. But they had both inherited Patrick's arrogance and temper, and neither liked to be the loser in any verbal encounter they had; Patrick had cured them of physical arguments while they were both still boys, making them punch it out until they both collapsed. Grant looked as if he wouldn't mind a rematch right now!

Nathan shrugged. 'I don't think she'll want you to take her,' he explained truthfully.

Grant's mouth set in a mutinous line. 'It's my damned baby too! And I——'

'Grant, I really think Nathan is right about this,' she tried to soothe.

He turned blazing eyes on her. 'I might have known you would say that, you always side with Nathan!'

The inaccuracy of that made her give a choked laugh; she and Nathan never agreed about anything!

'It's always been the two of you versus the rest of the world.' He ran an impatient hand through his already tousled hair. 'I don't know why you don't just get married and to hell with it,' he scowled.

'Grant!' Nathan grated harshly.

'I know,' his brother scorned. 'A taboo subject. Maybe it isn't such a good idea; look how my "ideal" marriage is turning out!'

Brenna could have wept for his bitterness, wishing he and Lesli would just *talk* to each other.

'Grant, I think you're still drunk,' Nathan told him coldly. 'Either sober up or go to bed!'

His brother's chest heaved raggedly. 'I am sober; that's the problem. It all looked better when I was drunk.' He looked at Brenna with bloodshot eyes. 'Maybe your father had the right idea after all. He——'

'Grant!' Nathan's reprimand lashed out with all the force of a whip cracking, and Grant's head snapped back challengingly. 'Hurling insults at Brenna's father isn't going to help this situation,' he grated warningly.

'I wasn't insulting him,' Grant dismissed. 'I think he has the right idea; things look a hell of a lot rosier from the bottom of a whisky bottle.'

'You should know, you reached it last night,' Nathan rasped. 'You aren't fit to drive a car even if Lesli would agree to letting you take her to the doctor's!'

Grant scowled. 'Which she won't. I'm going for a ride—on horseback,' he caught Nathan's sharp look. 'If my wife feels like telling me how she and our baby are when she gets back perhaps you could let me know!'

Brenna watched him as he strode out of the house. 'He's really hurting,' she said regretfully.

'What do you expect?' Nathan bit out accusingly. 'Your sister is destroying him.'

Her mouth dropped open as she watched him stride away too, in the opposite direction to Grant. She had forgotten their own argument during the friction between him and Grant, but he obviously hadn't. She had a feeling Bill was going to see Nathan 'blow up' a lot more before she left here!

In the end Lesli only agreed to go to the doctor if Brenna accompanied her, although she insisted on going in alone when it came time for her to see Dan Whittaker.

Brenna glanced at Nathan as he idly flicked through a motoring magazine he had picked up from the table in front of them.

'Don't worry,' he drawled. 'She's going to be admitted.'

'I'm sure you're a powerful man, Nathan, and that your wishes will be considered, but——'

'It isn't a question of either of those things,' he rasped. 'Anyone can see Lesli is teetering on the edge of physical collapse.'

He was right, Lesli had looked even worse this morning, and because of that Brenna didn't believe for one moment that her sister's love for Grant was dead; their estrangement wouldn't be affecting her like this if it were. The same applied to Grant. She felt like knocking their heads together, although she doubted that would achieve more than heaping retribution on her head.

Nathan was also right about Dan Whittaker admitting Lesli, in fact he insisted she stay on right now, much to Lesli's annoyance.

'I don't have anything with me for a stay in hospital,' she protested to Nathan and Brenna.

'I can always drive back to the ranch and get your things while Nathan sees you settled in,' Brenna reasoned. 'I can be back in an hour.'

'I don't want to stay in hospital!' Lesli wailed.

Dan Whittaker looked at her reprovingly beneath bushy eyebrows; he was inclined to flabbiness about his middle, and was a good six inches shorter than Nathan; they seemed an unlikely pair to have become friends! 'Do you want this baby, Lesli?' he asked gently. 'Because I'm afraid if we don't get you rested up for a couple of weeks it's going to be born before it should. And even at seven months I can't guarantee it will survive.'

His shock tactics, although a little drastic, Brenna thought, seemed to have worked, for Lesli allowed the two men to see to her admission.

Brenna took the keys of the Camaro from Nathan's hand. 'Sure you trust me with it?' She attempted to lighten the strain that still existed between them.

'I trusted you with something infinitely more precious to me than my damned car,' he grated harshly. 'Try not to smash the car up too,' he jeered before going off with Lesli and Dan Whittaker.

Brenna paled at the raw anger in his accusation. But he hadn't given her his heart as he implied he had; he didn't have a heart to give.

'Well?' demanded Grant as soon as she got back to the ranch, looking a little better than he had earlier, and he hadn't been drinking again, despite his claim. 'Where's Lesli?' he frowned.

'The doctor has decided she should go into hospital—Grant, it's all right,' she assured him quickly as he paled. 'She needs to rest for a few weeks, get away from the friction that exists here at the moment,' she hastened to add as he was about to protest at the need for Lesli to do that in hospital when Mindy could have looked after her here.

'I have to go to her.' He picked up his car keys from the hall table.

Now he decided to talk to Lesli! 'I don't think that's a good idea, Grant——'

'I don't give a damn what you think,' he bit out. 'I wasn't asking your permission!'

'Do you give a damn about Lesli?' Her eyes flashed her own loss of patience.

'Of course I——'

'And the baby?'

'Not that argument again, Brenna,' he sighed. 'Lesli is my wife and that's my baby she's carrying; I have a right to be there!'

She couldn't argue with that right. 'Just let me get Lesli's case packed and we can go in together,' she encouraged softly.

His mouth twisted. 'I can assure you, I'm completely sober,' he told her.

'But you're upset,' she reasoned.

'All right,' he conceded with a sigh. 'But make it quick, will you?'

Brenna could feel his tension-filled gaze on her all the way down the hallway to the bedroom, and she quickly threw the things she thought necessary into a small case before hurrying back to join him. He was still standing in the hallway, looking as if he hadn't moved since she left him.

He took the case from her unresisting fingers, his expression grim as he threw it into the back of the car before putting out his hand for the keys.

'You drive like an old woman,' he rasped at her questioning look.

'At least we'll get there in one piece.' She ignored his hand, getting in behind the wheel of the gold vehicle.

'When?' The disgruntled Grant got in beside her. 'I'd like it to be today, if possible.'

Brenna clamped her lips together to hold back her angry retort; Grant was spoiling for a fight and she wasn't going to be his victim! Once they reached the hospital she realised that perhaps she should have let him take out his frustrated anger on her; it would have been preferable to the light of battle she saw in his eyes as they went into Lesli's room, and Lesli returned that look as she lay on top of the bed still fully clothed.

'Nathan?' Brenna questioned desperately.

'Talking to the doctor,' Lesli answered without looking at her, her angry gaze fixed on Grant. 'What are you doing here?' she demanded contemptuously.

'I've come to check on the welfare of my son.'

'*My* son,' Lesli interrupted tautly. 'Or daughter,' she added hardly.

'The baby is half mine.'

'How can you be sure of that?' she challenged.

'Lesli! Grant!' Brenna appealed for common sense. They both ignored her.

Lesli sat up. 'If you think I'm going to let this baby be used the way I was then——'

'I've never used you!' Grant stormed. 'I've *loved* you, but I've never used you!'

'Don't lie to me,' Lesli rasped. 'I know you for what you are now, and——'

'You know *me*, Lesli,' her husband thundered. 'And the things you're accusing me of just aren't true, and you know it!'

'You as much as admitted it!' Lesli shouted back. 'When I asked you you said——'

'That I knew what my father's will contained before he died,' he acknowledged harshly. 'That doesn't mean I admitted using you. I loved you, I would have married you anyway——'

'Would you?' Lesli scorned. 'I don't happen to think so.'

'I don't know who's been poisoning your mind like this, but——'

'No one "poisoned my mind",' she retorted. 'I just came to my senses. I—Oh!' Her face paled as she clutched at her lower abdomen, her face deathly pale.

'What is it?' Grant instantly forgot his anger at her obvious pain. 'Lesli!'

'It's the baby,' she gasped. 'Oh, my God, I think the pains have started. The doctor said it was too soon.' Her eyes were wide with panic.

'I'll go and get him.' Brenna rushed to the door.

'Grant?' She heard Lesli falter as she opened the door.

'It will be all right,' he instantly assured her. 'It will, Lesli.'

'Oh, please God!' her sister choked as Brenna hurried off down the corridor.

Her need to find the doctor and bring him to

Lesli was paramount, but she couldn't prevent the conversation between Lesli and Grant from going round and round in her mind. She knew why Lesli had run from Grant as she had now; it was the same reason she could never allow herself to love Nathan.

CHAPTER SIX

'LESLI was right.' Dan Whittaker joined Nathan and Brenna in the waiting-room where they had been since he began his examination. 'The baby has decided to come early.'

'Can't you do anything to stop it?' demanded Nathan.

His friend shook his head. 'It's too late for that.'

'Hell!' Nathan ran a frustrated hand through his hair. 'Grant ought to be horsewhipped!'

'I should never have brought him here.' Brenna let her breath out shakily.

Dan shook his head. 'It's really a culmination of things rather than just one,' he comforted. 'Lesli is very tired and run down; this could have happened at any time.'

'And the baby?' Brenna looked at him with shadowed eyes.

'We'll just have to wait and see,' he said noncommittally. 'At least she was in the right place when it happened.'

Brenna glanced sideways at Nathan once they were alone again. He hadn't given any sign of condemnation, and yet she *felt* as if he blamed her for what was happening—as she did. The only good thing to come out of this was that Grant was still in with Lesli. But now that she

realised the reason for Lesli's hurt and confusion
about her marriage, she wasn't sure how long that
would last. She couldn't understand what, after
four years of happy marriage, had happened to
make Lesli suspect Grant's motives the way she
obviously did.

She stood up to pace the room in impatient
movements. 'Well?' she frowned at Nathan. 'Why
don't you just get it over with?' She met his gaze
challengingly.

'Get what over with?' His voice was soft—too
soft as far as Brenna was concerned.

'If you're going to chew me out for the way I
let this situation build up, then I wish you'd get
it over with!' Her eyes flamed.

He shrugged broad shoulders, sitting forward
in his chair, his elbows resting on his knees, his
hands clasped together in front of him. 'I'm not.'

'Why aren't you?' she demanded, irritated by
his calm attitude.

He looked at her with narrowed eyes. 'My
"chewing you out" isn't going to help anybody.'

'No, but——'

'For God's sake, Brenna.' He stood up
forcefully. 'I'm not stupid enough to think you
could have stopped Grant coming here; Lesli
wouldn't have been able to prevent me getting
here if the positions had been reversed!'

Nathan's baby. That had once seemed more
than a possibility to her, and thinking of it again,
here and now, caused a warmth of emotion inside
her that made her sway towards him.

'Whoever my wife happened to be,' he added

harshly, his hands thrust into his denims pockets now.

Brenna dragged herself back from the insanity of putting her arms about him. Minutes ago she had learnt that Lesli suspected what she had always known; that the Wade brothers were willing to sacrifice anything to hold on to full control of what they believed to be theirs: the ranch, the foothold of the Wade dynasty. Patrick might have appeased his own conscience by dividing it up between them the way that he had, but Grant and Nathan hadn't been willing to meekly sit back and accept it. She knew Grant did love Lesli, probably as much as a Wade was capable of loving; she had seen his love for his wife during their four years of marriage. But she also knew that possession of the ranch entered into his feelings. And she had known Nathan's proposal to her had been made for exactly the same reason, and was not motivated by love at all.

'You do realise that if anything should happen to this baby, the way things stand between them at the moment, it will be the end for Lesli and Grant?' Nathan suddenly rasped.

She dragged herself back from the hellish memories of knowing Nathan had only asked her to marry him because of the ranch, the physical attraction he felt for her being an added bonus as far as he was concerned. She swallowed hard as the realisation of what he had just said sank in. 'You don't mean . . . oh, *no!*' she groaned shakily.

His arms closed protectively about her. 'It's a possibility that has to be faced. You heard Dan earlier, even though the baby is seven months along he can't offer any guarantees.'

If the baby died it would destroy Lesli and Grant, and no matter what Lesli said to the contrary, she loved Grant more than anything else in the world, and always had. Without the baby they both wanted so much the marriage couldn't survive, not now.

'It will be all right,' Brenna's voice was muffled against Nathan's chest. 'It has to be!'

Nathan put her away from him, his expression grim. 'I have to call Mindy and let her know what's happening——'

'Let me do that,' she cut in quickly, wiping the tears from her face.

He nodded abruptly. 'I think she would appreciate that.'

The frost left Mindy's manner as she put in a few abrupt questions during Brenna's halting explanation of what was happening.

'Give Lesli my love when you see her,' Mindy spoke huskily. 'And tell Grant—tell Grant——'

'I understand,' she said softly as the elderly woman's voice broke emotionally. 'I'll call you again as soon as—as soon as we know anything.'

But they didn't know anything 'soon'. The labour was prolonged, the day stretching into evening before a haggard-looking Grant came out of the delivery room.

'We have a daughter,' he choked. 'She's beautiful; black-haired, blue-eyed. And she may not last the night!' He swayed on his feet, his eyes squeezed tightly shut as tears streaked the hardness of his cheeks.

'Lesli?' Brenna prompted faintly.

He blinked, focusing on her with effort. 'She's very tired, but Dan's sure she's going to be fine.'

'Can we see her? Is——'

'Brenna!' Nathan cautioned harshly, his arm going about his young brother's shoulders. 'Sit here with Brenna for a while, and I'll go and have a word with Dan myself.'

'Yes.' All the fight had momentarily gone out of Grant, and he allowed himself to be seated, Brenna sitting quietly at his side while Nathan went in search of the doctor.

'She's so little,' Grant finally choked. 'So tiny, Brenna.' He blinked back the fresh tears. 'God, if she lives, and Lesli still wants to divorce me, I'll let her go. Anything, as long as the baby is allowed to live!' he vowed fiercely.

'You—you would let Lesli take the baby with her?' Brenna frowned.

He nodded. 'They let Lesli hold her, just for a second,' his face softened at the memory. 'She was crying and laughing at the same time, already she loves her deeply; yes, I'll let her take the baby with her if she really wants a divorce,' he rasped.

'And you?' Brenna prompted huskily. 'What will you do if that happens?'

He gave a scornful laugh. 'What is it you always said about the Wade men: they'll survive no matter what? I'll survive this too!' he claimed fiercely. 'God, if only she weren't so damned small,' he choked, his face in his hands. 'She wasn't much bigger than this, Brenna.' He held a hand up in front of him. 'How can such a tiny thing win the battle to live!'

If Grant were willing to let Lesli and the baby leave him then she had seriously misjudged how deep his love for Lesli went; he must love them both very much, enough to let them go.

'She's a Wade, Grant,' she told him firmly. 'And Wades don't quit.'

His smile was bitter. 'I just may do that if I lose either of them!'

There was no doubting his sincerity, and Lesli had to be made to see, even if they should lose their beautiful daughter, that the two of them still had a marriage to work at.

'We called her Christiana, after the two grandmothers,' Grant spoke again. 'But maybe the name will have more significance than we know.'

'Grant, don't,' she squeezed his arm. 'It *has* to be all right.'

He drew in a ragged breath. 'I wish I could believe that, but if you could see her——!' He shook his head, his eyes bleak.

'Lesli is asleep.' Nathan strode back into the room. 'We can all go and take a look at the baby in her incubator before we leave.'

'I'm not going anywhere,' Grant grated as he stood up to flex his tired shoulder muscles. 'I'll sit in with Lesli. If—if there's any news about Christiana I want to be with Lesli when they—when they tell her.'

'Dan's pretty hopeful, Grant,' Nathan soothed. 'She's small, yes, but she's quite strong.'

'Strong' hardly described the doll-like baby who lay asleep in the incubator; she was so tiny and still that Brenna couldn't believe she was real, fascinated as she saw a movement of one of the tiny hands. Grant was right, Christiana looked too tiny to survive. Tears wet her own cheeks.

'Dan thinks it best if we don't disturb Lesli again tonight,' Nathan spoke gruffly as they all stood outside Lesli's room. 'There's nothing more you can do here tonight, Grant, and——'

'I'm staying,' he repeated challengingly. 'Alone.'

'Grant, you——'

'Think in reverse, Nathan,' Brenna cut in softly, holding his angry gaze until it softened to understanding.

'I'll be out first thing in the morning, Grant,' he squeezed his brother's shoulder. 'Call if there's any news before then,' he instructed briskly. 'I doubt if either Brenna or I will be asleep.'

She knew that both of them wished they could have stayed at the hospital with Grant, but they had to respect that it was a vigil he had to keep alone.

'Nightcap?' Nathan suggested once they had told Mindy what was happening at the hospital and she had gone to bed after Brenna had assured her she could cook them something to eat if they should discover they were hungry.

'Please,' she accepted the brandy he handed her, its fiery warmth easing the numbness they both felt. 'Would you like me to get you something to eat?' she offered.

He shook his head. 'I'm not hungry.'

She gave a ragged sigh. 'Nor me. Do you think it's going to be all right, Nathan?' She looked at him pleadingly, never needing his strength as much as she did at that moment.

'I don't know,' he surprised her by admitting. 'I looked at that little girl battling for her life, and I—God, I didn't know babies could be that small!' he said shakily, taking a swallow of the brandy, wincing as it burned a path to his stomach. 'Did you notice how much like you she looked?'

Her startled gaze met his pained one. 'Nathan . . .?'

He shook his head. 'Until I saw her, Lesli's pregnancy had seemed a little unreal. Oh, I could see she was getting bigger, but . . . when I looked in that incubator and saw Christiana! She looked like you,' he rasped. 'And if she dies it will be as if a part of you died!'

'Nathan, no!' Brenna put her glass down to go to him, her arms about his waist as she put her head against his rapidly moving chest.

He gripped the tops of her arms. 'We could have had a baby like that!'

Her face paled as she was forced for the second time that day to think of Nathan's baby. She felt that warmth again at the thought of it.

'God, I need you tonight.' Grey eyes searched the pale beauty of her face. 'Sleep with me tonight, Brenna!' he urged.

She wanted that too, wanted to be held by him, loved by him, as they both sought oblivion during the long night hours. She gave a wan smile. 'My room or yours?' she invited huskily as he had that night so long ago.

'It doesn't matter which,' he shook his head. 'As long as you're with me.'

It wasn't a time for questioning motives, on either side, tonight they needed each other, and Brenna was prepared to lose the rest of her heart to this man for that need.

They watched each other as they undressed in Nathan's bedroom. Nathan was more muscular than ever, deeply tanned by the Alberta summer sunshine. His eyes darkened as Brenna unbuttoned the front of her blouse and let it fall to the floor before taking off the pale cream camisole that was all that covered her rose-tipped breasts, his hands the ones to unzip her skirt and let that fall to the floor too, her last piece of clothing, a tiny scrap of lace, quickly joining the pile of clothes.

Strong, roughened hands gently caressed her hips and thighs as Nathan's lips parted hers in a drugging kiss. His hair felt silky and crisp as her fingers laced through it, his body curved sensuously into hers as she felt the leap of desire in his thighs, gasping her pleasure as his lips and tongue moved purposefully to capture her breast.

Their need for each other was as primitive as life itself, as elemental as they each possessed the other in driving need.

She was ready for him, accepting him inside

her like a part of herself, the joy of being joined
to him in this way superseding all other thoughts
in her mind as they moved together in fierce
desire.

Flames licked at her body in a burning
crescendo, and she knew Nathan was consumed
by the same fire, hearing him call out her name as
they reached the peak of that desire together.

Nathan buried his face in her throat as his lips
burnt her flesh. 'It's always so perfect with you,'
he groaned. 'I've never known this with any
other woman.'

Physically they were unique; she had known
that a year ago even as she knew it now, it was
over every other basic requirement of a relationship that they disagreed. 'Let's not talk,
Nathan,' she encouraged.

'No,' he acknowledged ruefully. 'Things always
get messed up when we talk!'

Neither of them made any attempt at conversation during the night hours, the only sounds from
within the capacious bed were small gasps and
murmurings of pleasure. Sleep was unnecessary
as they reacquainted themselves with each other's
bodies, and it was almost six o'clock when Brenna
suggested going back to her own room.

'What for?' His arms tightened about her.

To put her tattered defences back together!
Admittedly there had been no talk of marriage
between them this time, no mention of anything
beyond the moment, but she no more trusted
Nathan now than she had a year ago.

'I thought we could have breakfast and go back

to the hospital,' she dismissed lightly, once again drawn to him as he looked boyishly handsome with his hair ruffled in the early morning light.

'Brenna?' He grabbed hold of her arm as she would have got out of bed. 'Is this going to happen again?' His eyes were dark.

She avoided that gaze. 'No.'

'Brenna!'

Her fingers faltered as she drew the camisole over her head, and then she completed the task. 'Just last night, you said, Nathan.' She concentrated on fastening her clothes.

'Damn you!' he stood up. 'You know I want you for more than one night!' he glared.

She looked at him with unflinching eyes. 'I *can* explain last night, Nathan,' she bit out. 'The newest member of our family, a tiny baby,' her voice was husky, 'is fighting for her life. Last night we needed to reassure ourselves of our own survival, and we did it in the most fundamental way there is!'

He closed his eyes, running a hand over them in weary acceptance of the truth. 'Go and get dressed,' he instructed harshly. 'We may as well drive in to the hospital together.'

Tears joined the water cascading down her cheeks as she took a shower in her own bathroom. Last night she had proved more than life with Nathan, she had proved once and for all that she loved him. She always had. It wasn't even difficult to pinpoint the time she had realised that she loved him, had recognised it—and as quickly buried it!—after arriving home from a date when

she was eighteen. For once she had been early.
Gary Brody had been one of her more persistent
dates as he tried to persuade her that everyone
made love after their first few dates nowadays.
She was growing tired of his persistence and had
ended the evening abruptly, then sat talking to
Nathan for over an hour once she got in,
suddenly realising that she would rather spend a
few minutes just talking with him than a whole
evening with Gary or anyone else. She had gone
to college in England knowing she loved Nathan,
and even the pretence she had given herself that
something might one day come of those feelings
had been quickly shattered. She might have told
her heart to stop loving him, it just hadn't been
listening!

It still wasn't listening.

CHAPTER SEVEN

GRANT called while Brenna was in the shower; Christiana was doing well, and Dan was very optimistic!

Lesli was awake when they arrived at the hospital; she had been allowed to get up and be taken in a wheelchair to look at her daughter. Lesli and Grant sat holding hands during Brenna and Nathan's visit, their love for their daughter superseding everything else at this moment.

Brenna longed to talk to her sister alone, to assure her of the depth of Grant's love. Maybe when they had first married his prime objective had been to hold the ranch together, but he loved Lesli with everything now; he couldn't have offered to let her and the baby go out of his life if he didn't.

But it was impossible to talk to Lesli that day. Grant was always at her side, Nathan always hovering in the background. But she would talk to her sister very soon, would explain about Grant's reaction last night; Lesli couldn't possibly doubt him after that.

But 'very soon' never seemed to materialise. She visited Lesli and Christiana every day, but Grant or Nathan or Mindy, or one of Lesli's friends from neighbouring ranches was always there too. By the time Christiana was two weeks old and gaining enough weight for Dan to think they might be able to discharge mother and baby in another couple of weeks, she still hadn't had the opportunity to talk to Lesli alone. But for now the married couple seemed to have forgotten their differences, and Grant was spending all the time that he could at the hospital.

When Brenna wasn't visiting Lesli and Christiana she was up in her studio finishing the Koly illustrations. She was well within the schedule, having little else to do but disappear into the studio every evening after dinner, Nathan being either absent or busy in his study.

'I don't think you're taking care of Brenna, Nathan,' Lesli chided him one morning when they had both arrived within a few minutes of each other to visit her. 'She's looking pale,' she frowned.

Next to her sister perhaps she did look a little pasty; if the latter end of her pregnancy hadn't agreed with Lesli then motherhood certainly did. Lesli was glowing with health, secure in the knowledge that her daughter was thriving. But Brenna certainly didn't need to be subjected to Nathan's probing look, especially as it was the first time he had really looked at her in days.

His mouth twisted. 'Any man who tried to take care of Brenna would have to be a masochist—or worse,' he grated harshly.

'Maybe she's been working too hard.' Her sister still looked concerned.

He shrugged. 'I think Brenna is old enough to know when she should stop.'

'But——'

'Lesli,' Brenna cut in impatiently, 'I'm not pale, I'm not working too hard——'

'—and she certainly doesn't need me to take care of her,' Nathan finished tauntingly.

'Maybe she needs to get out and enjoy herself for a while,' Leslie continued to worry.

'The damned phone hasn't stopped ringing since she got home,' Nathan scowled. 'All her old boy-friends have heard she's back!'

Lesli's expression brightened. 'Was Gary one of the ones who called?'

'I think your maternal instinct must be working overtime,' Brenna dismissed indulgently. 'Poor Christiana will have her husband picked out for her before she's out of her cradle!'

'Not if I have anything to do with it,' Grant cut in fiercely, a look of uncertainty crossing his face as he realised what he had said. 'I mean——'

'Look, if it will make you feel any happier, Lesli,' Nathan drawled, 'I'll take Brenna out to lunch and feed her up.'

Ordinarily Brenna would have told him what he could do with his lunch, but she realised it had been a way of covering up the moment of awkwardness as Grant realised he might not have 'anything to do' with Christiana's growing up and eventually finding a husband, and also a way of getting them both out of the room so that the married couple could talk in private if they wanted to. She hoped they did.

'Just for that you can take me to any vegetarian restaurant you like,' she challenged, the fact that she knew he preferred an omnivorous diet making her mischievous. Nathan couldn't stand any sort of completely meatless menu—it had been a constant argument between them in the old days. She knew by the light of battle in his eyes that today was going to be no different.

'You'll be eating on your own, then,' he told her as he opened the door for her. 'I had in mind a decent restaurant, not some gathering-place for leaf-eaters!'

'Take me to Mother Tucker's, then,' she amended, hearing Grant and Lesli chuckle together as she and Nathan left. She relaxed a little once they were outside. 'Poor Grant,' she sighed. 'I could have cried for him!'

'Yes,' rasped Nathan, his hands thrust into his trouser pockets as he walked at her side. 'He still refuses to tell me what it's all about,' he scowled, his teasing mood gone now that he didn't have an audience.

Brenna avoided his gaze. 'Then it must be private to them,' she dismissed.

'Hm,' he acknowledged unconvincingly. 'Do you think they'll make it?'

'Yes,' she answered without hesitation. 'Because they love each other.'

'Where are you going?' Nathan frowned as she walked off towards the pick-up she was using during her stay. 'I thought we were going for lunch.'

She turned to look at him. 'That was just for Lesli and Grant's benefit.'

'Maybe,' he conceded. 'But it wouldn't hurt for us to have lunch together.'

'Why?' she frowned suspiciously.

'Why not?' His eyes narrowed. 'We both seem to have been too busy to talk lately.'

'Talk?' she echoed, startled. 'We don't have anything to talk about.'

'Grant and Lesli?' he rasped. 'And Christiana. You can't stop being a member of this family just because you would like to, you know.'

She flushed at the accusation. 'I haven't——'

'And whether you like it or not I'm a member of this family too!'

'I know that,' she snapped, wondering how he supposed she could ever forget it.

'Then don't you think there's already enough friction between Lesli and Grant without us being at each other's throats?' he sighed.

'That's all this is?' she hesitated, having avoided him since the night Christiana had been born.

His mouth twisted derisively. 'The fact that I accept every time you offer your body to me may have given you an inflated opinion of your own attraction, but I can assure you I'm not about to leap on you at the least provocation; certainly not in a crowded restaurant!'

Brenna blushed at his insulting tone—as she knew she was supposed to do. But he was right, she was the one who offered her body; he was hardly the type to force a woman. He had never needed to!

'If we're going to put up a united front, Nathan,' she rasped, 'I suggest you put those two nights out of your mind.'

He gave a derisive snort. '*You* must be out of your mind if you think I can do that!'

Her blush deepened. 'This isn't going to work, Nathan.'

'I'm sorry,' he sighed, grabbing her arm as she would have turned away from him. 'Let's compromise; I won't forget them, but I won't talk about them either. Hm?' he encouraged.

Green eyes warred with grey until finally Brenna nodded in weary agreement; trying to avoid him and, consequently, memories of their nights together, was proving too much of a strain anyway.

They lunched at Mother Tucker's, one of the leading restaurants in the city, talking of impersonal things, and Brenna relaxed to such an extent that she even began to fool herself she was having a good time. Nathan *could* be charming when he felt the need, and at the moment he felt the need. Maybe it was because of that relaxed charm he exuded that she noticed the exact moment his mood changed, following his gaze towards the restaurant entrance.

A couple were just entering, the man short and middle-aged, obviously dazzled by his companion, a tall, willowy blonde with eyes the colour of the amber jewels she wore about her slender throat, the rich gold of her dress giving her a glow, although her beauty would have stood out no matter what she wore.

Brenna had no need for anyone to tell her this was the beautiful Dee Wallace, the woman Nathan had been dating for the last two or three

months. The woman was such a complete
contrast to her in looks that she couldn't help
wondering how Nathan had come from this
woman's arm to her own.

The couple were seated at a table across the
room from them, and the woman looked about
her interestedly once they had ordered their
drinks, her eyes glowing like gold as she spotted
Nathan, although she frowned a little as she saw
Brenna, making her excuses to the man she was
dining with before getting up to come over to
their table.

'Nathan,' she greeted huskily, bending down to
brush her reddened lips against his, then
straightening to look curiously at Brenna as
Nathan returned the caress.

Nathan stood up. 'Dee, this is my stepsister,
Brenna Jordan. Brenna, Dee Wallace.'

My lover, Brenna silently added the description
he hadn't. Standing together as they were,
the two of them exuded physical intimacy, Dee's
body lightly resting into Nathan's in soft
compliance.

Dee gave a friendly laugh. 'For a moment I
thought I should feel jealous of you,' she
confided. 'I was ready to scratch your eyes out,'
she admitted ruefully.

'That won't be necessary,' she drawled curtly.

'You're English.' The golden eyes widened.

'I did say stepsister, Dee,' Nathan rasped.
'Even after ten years Brenna still hasn't lost her
English accent.'

'It's very attractive,' Dee frowned.

'Would you and your friend like to join us, Miss Wallace?' Brenna offered tautly.

The other woman shook her head regretfully. 'This is a business lunch, I'm afraid. Perhaps another time,' she dismissed. 'See you tonight, darling?' she smiled warmly at Nathan.

'Yes,' he said abruptly.

Dee gave him another lingering kiss. 'Nice to have met you, Brenna,' she smiled.

Brenna handed Nathan a napkin as soon as the other woman had left. 'You have lip-gloss on your top lip,' she mumbled, unable to look at the spot where the dark lip-gloss stood out conspicuously against his tanned flesh.

Anger flared in dark grey eyes as he roughly removed the offending mark.

'She's your lover,' Brenna stated flatly.

'Yes,' he bit out viciously, crumpling the napkin before slowly letting it fall on to the table.

'She's beautiful.'

'Yes,' he ground out.

Maybe she would have felt better if she could have disliked the other woman, but she couldn't; she had found Dee Wallace as beautiful and charming as Mindy's obvious admiration of her had implied her to be; Mindy couldn't stand anyone with affected airs and graces.

'Damn it, Brenna,' Nathan grated suddenly, 'I wouldn't need to go to other women if you——'

'No!' she cut in harshly. 'Don't say it, Nathan,' she choked.

'No,' he sighed raggedly. 'You're right, it will serve no purpose. Are you ready to leave?'

She had been ready for the last ten minutes. She wished she had never met Dee Wallace, and she had to acknowledge that she was a beautiful and likeable woman. And that she was Nathan's lover.

Far from smoothing things over between them that lunch seemed to be another thing that stood between them. Now when Nathan drove off in the evenings and often didn't return until the morning Brenna knew to whom he was going and why. She couldn't work on those evenings he went to see Dee Wallace, and finally, in an act of desperation, she accepted a dinner invitation from Gary Brody.

At eighteen she had thought him wonderfully sophisticated at two years her senior. But somewhere along the way the two years had ceased to matter, and in fact at twenty-four Gary now seemed younger than she was.

The evening should have been fun, she and Gary meeting up with a group of her old friends at a bar in the city after they had had dinner together, talking and laughing with the happy group until almost midnight.

She knew when Gary chose to drive the Cochrane way back to the ranch that he intended parking before taking her home; the steep hill before they reached the small town of Cochrane was one of their old parking spots.

'Remember this place?' Gary grinned at her as he turned off on to the gravel road.

'Yes. Look, Gary, I think I should go straight home tonight——'

'That's crazy,' he dismissed, parking so that they could look down on the brightly lit town of Cochrane with its four thousand population. 'It's a clear evening,' he remarked with satisfaction as his arm moved about her shoulders.

Brenna could have screamed with the stupidity she had shown in accepting this invitation tonight. She hadn't parked out like this since she was eighteen! 'It's lovely,' she acknowledged impatiently. 'Look, Gary——'

'I've missed you, you know,' he told her intensely. 'I've never been able to understand why you had to go to college in England.'

'Because I am English,' she pointed out drily.

'Yes, but——'

'Gary, would you please take me home?' she said tautly. 'I have a headache, and—Gary!' she protested as he moved determinedly towards her.

'You always were the most beautiful girl I've ever seen,' he caressed the side of her mouth before claiming her lips in a punishing kiss. 'Brenna. Oh God, Brenna!' he groaned.

'Gary, stop this!' she ordered, pushing him away. 'Stop it, damn you!'

'What's the matter with you?' He looked at her accusingly. 'We're both adults now,' he complained.

'We certainly are,' she agreed stiffly. 'And past the age of making love in a car!'

'We could always go to a motel.'

'No, Gary,' she glared.

He flushed. 'What's the matter, Brenna, are you too stuck up for your old friends now?'

What was the matter was that Nathan had made it impossible for her to respond to any man but him! 'You know that isn't true, Gary,' she reproved softly. 'The trouble is that you are a friend, and I can't think of you in any other way. Now would you please take me home?'

She wasn't at all surprised when he didn't suggest seeing her again, knowing his pride was injured because she didn't see him in a romantic way. But she couldn't force a desire that came all too easily with Nathan.

'Nightcap?'

She looked up sharply as Nathan spoke to her, silhouetted in the doorway of the dimly lit lounge. He had left the house before her this evening, and she had supposed he was going to see Dee; she hadn't thought he would be back yet. 'Yes,' she accepted his offer gruffly.

'It's only coffee, I'm afraid.' He raised dark brows questioningly.

'Coffee will be fine,' she nodded, having already had enough alcohol this evening.

'Bad evening?' Nathan sat across from her as she drank the strong brew.

She shrugged, closing her eyes wearily. 'I sent off the Koly story and illustrations today, and I thought it would be nice to go out and celebrate; getting groped in the front seat of a car isn't my idea of a celebration!'

'Gary?' he demanded.

His tension was a tangible force across the room, and Brenna raised her head to look at him. 'It was my own fault,' she sighed. 'I shouldn't have gone out with him.'

'No, you shouldn't,' he rasped as he stood up.

'Nathan?' she blinked as he came to stand over her.

'I had a lousy evening too,' he murmured raggedly, pulling her up to stand in front of him. 'In fact, all my evenings have been lousy lately,' he added grimly.

'Dee . . .?'

'Isn't you,' he bit out. 'I'm sick of going to another woman for what I want from you!' He moulded her body against his.

'Nathan, we can't . . .!'

'Who the hell says we can't?' His eyes glittered angrily. 'I'm only happy lately when I'm with you; arguing with you, making love with you, being hated by you. God, I can even stand the first and last as long as I can have the second,' he groaned. 'I don't want to go to another woman any more, Brenna, I want *you*. And I know you want me too.'

How was it possible to deny wanting a man when your body was melting against his of its own free will, when your breathing was suddenly laboured, when you couldn't break your gaze away from his?

'Nathan, I can't,' she managed to choke. 'Please don't make me.'

For a moment he stared down at her in angry silence, then he pushed her away from him. 'Perhaps one day you'll tell me why you're putting us both through this,' he ground out. 'Because I sure as hell don't understand it!' He stormed out.

'Neither do I!'

Brenna's control broke as she turned to confront Mindy, rushing into the other woman's arms as she held them open to her. She couldn't seem to stop the tears once they had started, and Mindy seemed content to let her cry until there were no more tears left.

'Now,' Mindy sat her down firmly, sitting next to her. 'Why are you constantly pushing Nathan away when you love him?'

'I don't——'

'Don't lie to me, Brenna,' the other woman reprimanded. 'I've known you too many years not to know when you're lying,' she added sternly. 'I know that you love him, and I know that he cares for you too.'

'No!'

'Brenna, I just heard him tell you how much he wants you. And to a man a want as fierce as that one, can only mean love, even if he doesn't come right out and call it that. I'm not quite senile, you know,' Mindy reproved. 'I've had my own share of relationships with men in my time.'

'Oh, Mindy, I'm sure you have,' said Brenna between a sob and a laugh. 'You don't understand.'

'I've just told you I don't,' the housekeeper conceded. 'I don't understand any of you. Lesli and Grant have been in love with each other ever since I can remember, and yet she walked out on him when she's expecting his baby, *you* spent a night with Nathan before running off to England and not coming back.' She shook her head. 'I think you've all gone mad.'

'Maybe a little,' Brenna agreed.

'You aren't going to stay here and marry Nathan this time either, are you?'

'No,' she shook her head.

'And will Lesli be staying with Grant?' Mindy frowned her confusion.

Brenna nodded. 'If I have anything to do with it, yes,' she said determinedly.

'Do you have any idea why she left in the first place?'

Brenna avoided the older woman's gaze. 'I have a good idea.'

'Then I hope you can stay long enough to sort this mess out,' Mindy shook her head exasperatedly. 'Because tiny and vulnerable as she is, Christiana is going to need both her parents for a long time to come, not just one.'

'I'm going to do the best I can to see that she keeps them both,' she assured her.

'And after that I suppose you'll leave poor Nathan again?' Mindy reproved.

'I've never been *with* him, so my leaving can hardly be classed as leaving *him*,' Brenna protested.

Mindy sighed. 'I know I've been a little rough on you since you got back . . . all right, more than a little,' she corrected at Brenna's sceptical look. 'But you didn't see Nathan last summer when you didn't come home; I did!' she added grimly.

'Mindy, sometimes things aren't always what they seem to be . . .'

'You and Lesli have been able to lead Nathan and Grant a merry dance ever since you first came here, there's no mistaking that,' the other woman said drily. 'And I don't suppose it will ever change.'

'I shall be leaving soon, Mindy,' she teased. 'Then you can have your peace and quiet back.'

'I prefer it when Nathan is ranting and raving; at least that way I know he's alive!'

'Mindy, he'll be all right. Nathan is always all right,' Brenna added bitterly.

'Oh, I'm not saying he won't survive,' the other woman frowned. 'But with you gone he could just fall into the clutches of someone like Dee Wallace.'

Brenna's brows rose mockingly, although the thought of Nathan married to Dee gave her a sick feeling in the pit of her stomach. 'I thought you liked and approved of Miss Wallace,' she mocked.

'In preference to you, never!' Mindy stated emphatically. 'But I won't sit back and let you hurt him a second time.'

'I won't,' she said with certainty, sure Nathan couldn't *be* hurt.

The older woman sighed heavily. 'But you're going to let Dee Wallace get him on the rebound?'

'I thought you wanted him to be happy!'

'With you, not with Dee Wallace!'

'I'm sorry,' Brenna shook her head. 'I happen to think enough Jordans have already married into this family.'

'You're a fool, Brenna,' Mindy said sadly. 'There were never two people more made for each other than you and Nathan.'

Her mouth quirked as she tried to keep the conversation light. 'I'm sure Romeo and Juliet wouldn't agree with you, nor Antony and Cleopatra either. Or Jane Eyre and Mr Rochester, for that matter.'

'Very funny, Brenna,' Mindy glared. 'But for all your flippancy you're going to regret that you've let Nathan slip away from you.'

She already regretted it. Wasn't half a relationship better than none at all? She hadn't thought so a year ago; but did she still feel the same way?

CHAPTER EIGHT

'SHE won't break, Nathan,' Lesli teased him.

'She's still so small,' he complained, holding Christiana as if she were made of glass.

Yesterday Grant had driven mother and baby home, and at a month old Christiana weighed a healthy five pounds, although as Nathan said, she did still seem very small. But her lungs made up for her lack of size, as all the household had heard during the night, her cries waking everyone, although Lesli was obviously used to the disturbed nights now and looked the freshest of the four of them. Christiana was now sleeping like a little angel!

Brenna watched Nathan holding the little baby, her heart aching at how right he looked with Christiana in his arms. He would be a good father to his children. Unfortunately, she wouldn't be their mother.

Or would she? Something that should have happened a week ago hadn't. They had got away with their lovemaking a first time, she wasn't so sure they were going to be as lucky a second time. It still seemed too tentative to be true, although she could feel the anticipation building up inside her just at the thought of it. It was too soon to mention the possibility to Nathan yet, although she knew if it were true she wouldn't keep it from him.

And he did look so right holding Christiana.
'Your turn.'

She blinked up at him as he held out
Christiana to her. She had held the baby dozens
of times in the hospital, but somehow the act took
on a new meaning now, and tears filled her eyes
as she gazed down at the beautiful little face
beneath the mop of silky black hair.

'She's going to break a few hearts when she's
older,' mused Nathan.

'Yes,' Grant agreed abruptly.

'We'll have to have a boy next so that he can
protect her,' Lesli put in huskily.

Brenna could have cried at the joy that flared in
Grant's eyes. The married couple had continued to
occupy separate bedrooms on Lesli's return home
yesterday, and obviously Grant had seen that as an
indication that Lesli still wanted to divorce him.
Mention of a brother for Christiana had to mean
that wasn't so—didn't it?

'Er—Nathan, you said something about going
out for a ride?' she prompted quickly, handing
the baby back to Grant as he continued to look at
Lesli.

A frown darkened Nathan's brow. 'What . . .?
Oh,' he nodded understandingly as he saw her
fierce expression. 'Of course,' he nodded drily,
opening the bedroom door for her. 'See you two
later.'

'I think they've already forgotten us,' Brenna
mocked as they walked outside into the sunshine.

'Probably,' he drawled. 'Does that mean our
ride is off?'

She looked up at him sharply. The two of them had once again been doing their best to avoid each other the last two weeks, and as a way of preventing arguments it had worked very well. She couldn't see him actually seeking her company now.

'Don't sound so disappointed, Nathan,' she said sarcastically.

He swung her round to face him as she would have walked off. 'But I am,' he assured her huskily.

Her eyes widened, then she frowned as she saw the flare of desire in his eyes. 'I thought you were still seeing Dee.'

'I am,' he rasped. 'Does that mean we can't go riding together? Is it me or yourself that you don't trust, Brenna?' he taunted as she hesitated.

Resentment flared in her eyes. 'I haven't exactly been beating a path to your bedroom door the last two weeks!' she snapped.

'That's probably because I haven't been in it,' he drawled. 'Or hadn't you noticed?'

Oh, she had noticed that he had spent most of his nights away from the ranch, and so had Mindy, from the reproving looks she gave him at the breakfast table each morning. Obviously his desire for Brenna didn't stop him going to the other woman for solace.

'Wasn't I supposed to?' she challenged mockingly.

His mouth tightened. 'Can you blame me for going to a woman I don't have to beg from?'

'You've never had to beg from me!' she defended.

'You would have liked to have me on my knees to you!' he grated.

No, she had never wanted that. She just wanted to leave here, go back to England, where she no longer had to see him. She had never wanted to punish him for what he was, knew he couldn't help being the way that he was, that he was a Wade.

'You're wrong, Nathan,' she told him softly. 'All I ever wanted was for you to leave me alone.'

'And now that I have?'

She hated it! She hated thinking of him spending his nights with Dee Wallace, making love to the other woman, as he would one day make love to his wife. But after seeing the way Lesli had been destroyed by the knowledge of Grant's mercenary behaviour she was even less sure she could ever settle for what Nathan offered.

She shrugged. 'It's your life.'

'God, you really don't care about anything, do you?' he rasped, his eyes cold.

'Then I must have become more of a Wade than I realised!' she scorned.

Nathan drew an angry breath into his lungs at the insult. 'Are you coming for a ride or not?' he bit out.

'Actually, I'm spending the day at the Brody ranch,' she revealed reluctantly.

'With Gary?' His eyes were narrowed.

'Yes,' she confirmed defensively.

'With the man who "groped you in the front seat of his car"!' Nathan rasped disbelievingly.

'Yes!'

'Whose idea was that?' he demanded tautly.

'Gary telephoned, and I——'

'And you aren't spending the day with *him*,' Nathan told her arrogantly.

'Don't tell me—Nathan, put me down!' Brenna protested as he picked her up and threw her over his shoulder in a fireman's lift. 'Nathan!' she squealed as he refused to put her down.

'You want to be groped in the front seat of a car—then I'll be the one doing the groping.' He threw her into the passenger seat of his car before getting in behind the wheel and accelerating away.

Brenna straightened just in time to see Bill grinning at them from the paddock, tilting his hat to her mockingly, his eyes twinkling merrily at the display of Wade arrogance he had just witnessed.

She turned furiously to Nathan. 'You've just made us a laughing stock!'

'I couldn't give a damn,' he bit out grimly, his eyes narrowed on the road.

'I could! You ... Where are we going?' she gasped as he turned towards Banff rather than Calgary.

He gave her a chilling glance. 'I'm taking you up into the mountains where the only people to hear your screams for help will be the animals!'

She gave him a scathing glance. It was the end of the summer season, but all the same there were still plenty of holidaymakers travelling up through the Rockies through Banff and Jasper; the number of caravans and campers that went that way every day was evidence of that. Nathan would be lucky if he could find somewhere there wasn't people.

If his anger had lessened on the drive from the ranch to Lake Louise there was no evidence of it from his tight-lipped profile, and as he took the less used turn-off for Moraine Lake Brenna's scorn turned to trepidation.

'Nathan . . .'

'Only the animals, remember?' he grated between clenched teeth.

She turned completely in her seat to look at him. 'Look, I wasn't spending the day alone with Gary, a group of us were going to laze around his pool, and . . . Nathan,' she chided impatiently as he looked unmoved by the revelation. 'This is ridiculous,' she sighed. 'You know how short-handed you've been at the ranch the last month with Grant at the hospital most of the time; you can't just take the day of like this.'

'I just did,' he drawled.

'This is all so silly——' She broke off at the fierce anger in his eyes as he turned to her. She swallowed hard. 'What are you going to do?'

'I've always had this fantasy of laying you down on the grass in the sunshine and making love to you. I'm about to fulfil it,' he ground out.

'Nathan, you can't just make love to me any time you feel like it,' she protested.

'You want it too,' he said confidently.

She must be so transparent to this man; the erotic picture he had painted with his fantasy had filled her with longing too!

He turned off the road on to what must be a
Rangers' track, the grass simply flattened down a
little where tyres had passed over it before,
although that didn't look as if it had happened
lately. It was a bumpy ride, and when Nathan
finally stopped the car Brenna realised they must
have gone about half a mile or more from the
main road, completely shielded from view by the
tall pine trees.

'Shall we walk?' he suggested.

'Walk?' she echoed uncertainly.

The anger had gone from his eyes and in its
place was a languid warmth. 'It's a long time
since I just walked in the mountains,' he said
huskily.

If walking was going to help him forget his
threat to 'grope' her then she was all for it. She
didn't feel quite as happy with the arrangement
when he took her hand in his as they walked
along, her heart lurching at the warm intimacy of
that calloused hand.

'I used to bring you fishing up here,' he
murmured, giving her a sideways glance. 'As I
recall, you didn't mind hooking in a fish for our
lunch!'

'That was because you told me they couldn't
feel any pain!' she glared.

'I think even a fish might notice it was being
eaten!' he dismissed that logic.

'Nathan——'

'This looks as good a spot as any.' He came to a
halt beneath a tall pine tree, the grass soft and
springy underfoot. 'The car idea was fine, but I

think I'm a little too old for it, and the Camaro is a little too cramped for what I have in mind for us.'

How could coldly calculating grey eyes be this warm, the pupils dilated to fathomless black; Brenna felt as if she were drowning in those fiery depths.

She sank down on to the grass with him, her arms about his neck as he bent over her to claim her mouth. They were in no hurry to do more than share languid kisses, had all the time in the world. The silk blouse Brenna wore moved easily over her head, her breasts were cream and honey to Nathan's avid mouth.

She loved the way he suckled against her, and wondered briefly if she carried his baby inside her, but only briefly—the erotically charged emotions soaring through her body were demanding complete control.

'Offer them to me, Brenna,' Nathan groaned raggedly, his mouth closing possessively over one turgid nipple as she cupped her breasts forward for his enjoyment. The fiery warmth shook her body, and she could feel herself ready for him, thrusting against him as his hand cupped her over lace.

'Not yet, my love,' he groaned as he peeled off her clothes piece by piece. 'This time I have to make you mine completely, until you realise that no other man can give you what I can ... No!' he protested raggedly as she began to draw away from him, his teeth rough against her hardened nipple. 'Only like this, Brenna,' he urged. 'Only like this!'

There was no doubting the truth of that, she had known it from the moment he first made love to her. And because she knew, as he did, that this was probably the last time they would touch like this, their lovemaking was wild, out of control, hurting even as they loved.

Nathan laid her naked on the warmth of his discarded shirt, feasting on her body like a man starved of food, drawing her inside the moist warmth of his mouth, and as that warmth touched the very centre of her womanhood she groaned her fevered need. It was a need Nathan answered, and her eyes glazed with passion when he at last moved above her.

'Nathan, please!' she urged as he rubbed sensuously against her.

'You take me!' he rasped.

She opened to him, engulfed him as she felt him shudder within her, the fevered movements of their bodies arching in rhythmic need. Brenna cried out her own release as, with a hoarse groan, Nathan flowed inside her in never-ending spasms.

He lay on his back at her side as they both gazed up at the clear blue sky through the branches of the majestic pine tree. 'No one but the animals,' he murmured in contentment.

Brenna felt too languidly replete to do more than limply rest her hand on the hard contour of his stomach. 'I didn't scream,' she said softly.

'Oh, yes.' He turned to smile at her. 'You screamed.'

She remembered now. As release shook her she had screamed her love for him.

'I love your body too, Brenna.' His hand cupped her breast, the nipple springing to life at the gentle caress of his thumb. 'I love what it does to me.'

Her gaze searched his face as he bent over her. Did he really believe she had only meant she loved his *body*? He was so intent on his ministrations to her breasts that it was difficult to read anything but desire in his face. So soon? Surely he couldn't want her again so quickly . . .?

He made love to her over and over again as they spent the day beneath the huge pine, taking, giving, letting himself be taken. Brenna lost all sense of time, aware only of Nathan and the beautiful ecstasy they could create between them.

'Cold?' Nathan gathered her close as she shivered. 'I guess fantasies don't allow for the fact that the summer is almost over and the evenings can be cold,' he grinned.

Fantasy. The closeness that existed between them now had to be part of that fantasy. And she didn't want it to end, had become a part of Nathan today, a part that she knew was as necessary to him as it was to her. He couldn't pretend *this* need for her!

'Hey!' he frowned as she rolled on top of him. 'More?' he groaned as he read the longing in her smoky-green eyes as she moved against him.

They both lay back exhausted after a climax more shattering than any other had shaken both their bodies, their hands entwined as the early evening air chilled their sweat-dampened bodies.

'I don't want you to catch pneumonia.' Nathan

sat up to help Brenna back into her clothes. 'If it isn't already too late!'

It was too late for her. She loved this man. All her efforts to escape that knowledge the last four years had been destroyed by this day of lovemaking. Maybe she wasn't meant to have everything in her life, certainly not a love that was without blemish. She knew Nathan wanted to marry her for the ranch, but after today how could she go on denying that she wanted him, or knowing how much he desired her? She hoped her father would forgive her, but she couldn't fight this love any longer, she needed Nathan too much to go on living without him!

'Brenna . . .?' Nathan touched the tears on her cheeks. 'Darling, I didn't think I'd hurt you! Sweetheart, I know I go a little insane when I have you in my arms, but—I'm sorry!' There was pain etched into his face. 'I just can't seem to stop making love to you once I start!'

'*Do* you love me, Nathan?' She desperately needed to hear the words, even if she knew it wasn't the complete love she felt for him.

His mouth tightened. 'That's a damned stupid question if ever I heard one!'

'*Do* you?' she prompted raggedly.

'I always have,' he grated, pulling on his own clothes. 'What is this, Brenna, some perverted idea of justice because you can't say no to me when we make love?'

'No,' she denied self-derisively, looking up at him tearfully. 'A need to know my feelings are at least returned a little!'

'Your feelings? Brenna?' He came down on his knees in the grass beside where she still sat. 'Brenna, talk to me!' he urged roughly.

'I meant it when I said I love you,' she admitted gruffly. 'I can't go on fighting it any more. I love you, and if you still want to marry me I . . . Yes,' she told him with simplicity.

'Yes?' he frowned.

'Yes, I'll marry you.'

'*What?*'

'You've changed your mind?' she said uncertainly. Maybe he had decided that with her lack of interest in the ranch she was no threat to him after all!

'Of course I haven't changed my mind,' he dismissed scornfully.

It was ridiculous to feel relief over something that she had always dreaded! 'I have,' she told him quietly.

'But . . . Never mind.' He shook his head. 'You'll marry me?' he said incredulously.

'Yes.'

'When?'

'When?' she gave him a startled look. 'But . . . I haven't had time to think about that,' she frowned.

Nathan pulled her to her feet, his hands lightly on her upper arms. 'I'm not giving you the chance to run out on me again,' he told her grimly. 'We get married as soon as I can make the arrangements. And if you have to go back to London in the meantime——'

'I do,' she put in quickly. 'There's the flat to sort out, and then there's Carolyn——'

'Then I come with you,' he stated arrogantly.

'That isn't necessary——'

'It's very necessary,' he told her intently. 'Last time you went to London alone, you didn't come back!'

'I promise you that I'll never run out on you again,' she looked up at him unflinchingly. After all, what could he do to her that was worse than marrying her for gain and convenience? But she had to accept that love for the ranch and keeping that together was the only love he could feel.

'I don't intend giving you the opportunity,' he told her forcefully.

'Nathan, I mean it—I can't run any more.'

He searched the unhappiness of her face. 'Brenna, we've just said we love each other, we're going to be married. Can't you tell me now what you've been running away *from*?' he frowned darkly.

'Isn't it obvious?' she dismissed with bravado, pride dictating that she couldn't bring out into the open the abhorrence she felt about being married for what she possessed and not because he loved her. 'You've always been so arrogant, Nathan,' she said lightly. 'But today I learnt that I only have to touch you to make you forget about that. I'm no longer afraid to marry you.'

'Afraid?' he echoed ominously. 'But—Brenna!' he groaned as she put her hand on his thigh, hardening beneath the gentle caress of her fingertips. 'It's too damned cold now to do that again here,' he rasped. 'But later tonight!' he promised huskily.

All she asked from this relationship was the

oblivion he could give her in his arms, knowing now that it was as necessary to her as the air she breathed and the food she ate. God, she had always known that, that was why she had feared being near him again!

She rested back against the head-rest on the drive back to the ranch, sensing Nathan's gaze on her often as she feigned sleep. She was no happier now that she had agreed to marry Nathan, but she knew that after today she would be even more miserable without him.

In the meantime she hoped Lesli and Grant had taken advantage of their absence from the ranch and solved at least part of their differences; Lesli had certainly seemed willing to do that earlier.

'Brenna?' A gentle hand shook her awake.

She woke with a start, straightening as she realised she had indeed drifted off into sleep and that they were now parked outside the house.

Nathan smiled at her, gently moving the hair back over her shoulder. 'I didn't mean to wear you out,' he teased lightly.

'I guess I'm not as practised as you,' she snapped, contrition instantly washing over her as she remembered she had agreed to marry him a short time ago. 'I'm sorry,' she frowned, finding it hard to shake off the old antagonisms. 'I didn't mean——'

'Brenna, I haven't touched Dee since you came back,' he told her quietly.

She searched his face disbelievingly, finding only honesty there. 'But all those nights——?'

'A hotel bed seemed preferable to knowing you were just up the stairs from my room,' he sighed.

'A hotel . . .? Nathan!' she groaned.

'I'm not denying I've spent my evenings with Dee,' he stated. 'But not the nights.'

'But—but she wants you!'

'She thinks because I've been leaving her at her door every night that there's someone else,' he shrugged. 'There's always been someone else! There haven't been as many women in my life as your friends thought, either; I don't go to bed with every woman I date, but I have made love to some of them,' he admitted. 'I was having a little difficulty accepting that it was my stepsister I really wanted,' he drawled. 'But in the end I was given no choice but to love you.'

Because of Patrick's will! Nathan was as good as admitting that now. Why not, she had always preferred honesty to deceit.

'Shall we go in and tell Lesli and Grant the news?' she suggested heavily.

'You're really going to go through with it this time?' he watched her closely.

'Really,' she nodded abruptly. 'I guess I belong here after all.'

'Bearing the dreaded Wade name?' he mocked.

'And the dreaded Wade children.' What choice did she have? She had run from him once, she didn't have the strength to do it again!

Nathan shook his head. 'I'm not sure I really believe this is happening.'

'You will,' Brenna drawled. 'Now let's go into

the house; we've already provided enough of a spectacle for one day!'

He chuckled as he came round to help her out of the car, his body pressing intimately down the length of hers as she leaned back against the closed door. 'I can't get enough of you!' he groaned his need as his mouth forged with hers.

'Are congratulations in order?'

Nathan raised his head to grin at a smiling Bill. 'They could be,' he drawled, looking down at a flushed-faced Brenna. 'They just could be.'

'Don't forget to invite me to the wedding.' Bill put his hand up by way of departure.

Nathan's arm moved about Brenna's shoulders. 'Let's go and tell Lesli and Grant, then maybe we can make it public.'

She felt a little as a condemned prisoner must once have done on his way to the hangman's noose; she knew there would be no escaping Nathan once he had announced their intention to marry. She hardly felt like a bride-to-be.

The house seemed very quiet, and Brenna realised that was probably because Mindy was in the kitchen preparing dinner, and Lesli was probably resting with the baby. Maybe Grant was even resting with them; he had certainly paced the floor of his lonely bedroom enough nights the last month!

'How could you do it?' snarled an angry voice in the silence. 'How the *hell* could you do it!'

Nathan had stiffened at her side, the warmth fading from his eyes as he looked at Grant. The younger man was very pale, lines etched beside his nose and mouth, an expression of disgust on his face.

'Grant, what the hell are you——'

'I thought I knew you, Brenna,' he rasped accusingly over Nathan's exclamation. 'I never thought you were capable of *this*!'

She moved instinctively against Nathan at the unexpected attack, her eyes wide.

'Grant!' Nathan bit out furiously. 'The fact that Brenna and I have spent the day together is none of your damned business! You——'

'But that letter is,' Grant stuck out his chin aggressively. 'And she wrote that—that garbage!' He looked fiercely at the stricken Brenna. 'You could have ruined my marriage with those *lies*!'

'Grant, will you explain yourself!' Nathan thundered.

'It's simple,' his brother ground out. 'My dear sister-in-law told Lesli that I only married her to get my hands on her share of this ranch!'

CHAPTER NINE

BRENNA knew she must have paled; she was having trouble breathing, stunned by the accusation. It was what she believed, yes, but she had never ever told Lesli that. And she couldn't remember anything in any of her letters sounding remotely as if she had.

'You're insane, Grant,' rasped Nathan. 'Worn out from the worry of the last month——'

'I'm not worn out,' Grant dismissed impatiently. 'I'm shocked, disgusted, bloody furious, but I am not insane or worn out.' He looked at Brenna with accusing eyes, calmer now, although no less angry. 'I've always loved you as a sister, and I thought you loved me in the same way.'

'I do!' she cried.

He shook his head. 'You deliberately set out to destroy me.'

'Grant, you know Brenna wouldn't do that,' Nathan bit out. 'Let's all go through to the lounge and talk about this calmly,' he suggested soothingly.

'I'm not feeling very calm right now,' Grant grated, but he preceded them into the lounge anyway.

'Now,' Nathan stood in front of the unlit fireplace while Brenna sat forward on the edge of the sofa and Grant paced the room in restless movements. 'Explain all this as clearly as you can,' he instructed his brother, his eyes narrowed.

'This morning Lesli told me the reason she walked out on me,' Grant revealed grimly.

'And you think it had something to do with Brenna?' Nathan said disbelievingly.

'I know it did,' he rasped. 'Do you realise she could have lost the baby, or died in the process herself, being told something like that?' he accused Brenna harshly.

'Grant, I didn't——'

'Of course it was you,' he dismissed disgustedly. 'Who else could it have been?'

'Grant, if Brenna says she doesn't know what you're talking about then I believe her,' rasped Nathan.

Blue eyes were turned on him pityingly. 'You've always believed everything she's told you! Tell him now, Brenna,' Grant jeered. 'Tell him you don't believe I married Lesli because she owned a quarter of the ranch?' He looked at her challengingly.

Her gaze slid away from his, and as quickly moved away from Nathan as she saw the uncertainty register in his face at her lack of a quick rebuttal. But how could she deny what she had always believed to be true? Although she didn't accept that it was anything she had written that had made Lesli believe it too.

'Brenna?' Nathan prompted harshly at her continued silence.

She swallowed hard, and she couldn't look up at either of them. 'I can't deny that,' she began gruffly. 'Because I——'

'You see?' Grant pounced triumphantly. 'My God, Brenna, you——'

'I never ever wrote and told Lesli how I felt,' she denied desperately. 'I wouldn't do that to her.' She shook her head. 'I love Lesli, I've never wanted to hurt her.'

'You believe Grant married Lesli because he didn't want to see any control of the ranch go out of the family?' Nathan said softly.

Brenna wasn't deceived by that softness, she could see the coldness in his eyes, the tension about his mouth. And she knew what he was thinking, could feel her chance of even a tentative happiness with him slowly slipping away.

And she knew why. She could see in that moment that she had misjudged him as badly as she had Grant, that he was stunned she could believe he and Grant would want the ranch that desperately. And she could see that he would never marry her now.

She felt as if someone had kicked her in the chest. Nathan had *never* wanted to marry her for the sake of the ranch, which meant he must have loved her all this time. It was a love that was dying through disillusionment. And she had killed it.

She wanted to go to him, to beg his forgiveness for believing such a thing could be true, but she could see by the coldness of his eyes that he wouldn't welcome her touch or her apology. He was as remote and removed from her now as he had been when she first arrived here ten years ago.

'Does Lesli believe I did this to her?' she asked Grant chokingly.

His mouth twisted derisively. 'Lesli doesn't believe you can do any wrong either,' he scorned. 'She's sure that you only meant to help her, not hurt her.'

'I have to go and see her.'

'I don't want you anywhere near her,' he grated harshly, barring her way. 'I want you to leave here now and never come back.'

'I've asked Brenna to be my wife,' Nathan put in flatly. 'She's accepted.'

Grant looked at him pityingly. 'You always were in love with her,' he sneered. 'I wonder what her reasons are for marrying you? After all, she wouldn't have you last time, would she? Maybe you were the next one to be destroyed?' he added scornfully. 'What were you going to do, Brenna, leave him at the altar? He would never have been able to hold his head up around here again!'

It was impossible to tell from Nathan's expression whether he believed what his brother was saying or not, but the mere fact that he wouldn't reveal his emotions to her was enough; he no longer trusted her with them!

She turned back to Grant. 'I promise you that I have no intention of hurting Lesli,' she said dully. 'I just want her to know that she must have been mistaken to ever believe I could have wanted to see her hurt.'

'And she'll believe you only meant it for her good,' he nodded grimly. 'Because she wants to believe that, because she loves you!'

'Grant . . .'

'If you upset her in any way, say anything else to poison her mind against me,' he ground out, 'I promise you, you'll regret it!'

Nathan stood in front of the window with his back towards the room as she went out to see Lesli, the taut set of his shoulders enough to tell her he believed Grant now, and that he wanted nothing else to do with her either.

Lesli was still asleep when she entered the bedroom, but from the happy flush to her cheeks her reunion with Grant had been all she could have ever hoped for. Christiana slept peacefully in her crib next to the bed, and as Brenna bent over to look at the downy-topped head she knew this was one of the last times she would be allowed on the ranch to see her and Lesli. It was no longer a question of her not wanting to come back here; she wouldn't be welcome.

She left Lesli still sleeping and went up to her studio, telephoning the airport and booking a seat out on the flight the next day before she began to pack her things, knowing she had lost the one man she could ever love. And he had loved her, not with the half-committed love of a Wade, but with an all-encompassing passion. And now it was dead.

'You're leaving?' Mindy stood in the doorway watching her pack. 'Now?' she frowned.

'You heard the argument,' Brenna sighed in realisation, wiping the tears from her cheeks.

'Who could help it?' the housekeeper drawled drily. 'Grant must have been shouting loud enough to have woken the dead!'

'Lesli and Christiana slept right through it,' sighed Brenna, unable to look at the other woman as she haphazardly packed her case.

'New mothers and young babies can sleep through anything—except the sound of each other's voice,' she mocked. 'But once Lesli does wake up, Grant is going to find himself in trouble; Lesli doesn't lose her temper very often, but when she does it's best to stand clear. And she's going to be more than angry when she finds out what Grant did to you.'

She shrugged. 'He thought he had the right.'

'And did he?'

'No!'

'So you're going to just pack up and run away from it all?'

Brenna sat down heavily on the bed. 'I haven't been given a choice.'

'You could still marry Nathan,' Mindy suggested gently.

'No,' she said self-derisively. 'He no longer wants to marry me.'

Mindy gave a snort of disbelief. 'He would want you if you'd committed murder!'

'In a way I've done just that; I've killed his trust,' groaned Brenna.

'Patrick should have got you all together and explained about his will,' Mindy shook her head. 'It's just caused confusion and misunderstanding.'

'It doesn't matter now,' Brenna sighed. 'I just have to talk to Lesli and then I'll be leaving. I'll stay at a hotel in town overnight.'

'A hotel?' Mindy sounded scandalised at the idea. 'This is your home——'

'No,' she denied sadly. 'I never allowed it to be that. And now it's too late to try. I'd prefer to stay at a hotel.'

'Grant is angry right now, but as soon as he comes to his senses——'

'I won't be here by the time that happens.' Brenna squeezed the other woman's hand reassuringly. 'Maybe it's all for the best.'

'I've never heard anything so damned stupid in my life.' It was evidence of how upset she was by the fact that she swore; Mindy never swore. 'You——'

'Mindy, if you don't mind I'd like to talk to Brenna. Alone.'

They both turned at the sound of that harsh request, Mindy taking one look at Nathan's coldly set face before joining him in the doorway.

'Now don't you start bullying her,' she reproved. 'Grant's already reduced her to tears!'

'I have no intention of bullying her,' he bit out tautly. 'I just want to talk to her.'

Brenna stared down at her hands once they were alone. She hadn't expected to see him again, for him to come to her like this, and she wondered what they could have left to say to each other. Goodbye, perhaps!

Nathan's hands were thrust into his denims pockets as he came further into the room. 'I just want you to know that I don't believe you wrote to Lesli so that she would leave Grant.'

Her eyes widened. 'You don't?'

'No,' he confirmed grimly. 'Above everything else you love Lesli. Her leaving Grant when she did might have been the time when he could be hurt the most; not only would he lose his wife, but also his child. But Lesli was hurt too, and I don't believe you would ever do anything to deliberately hurt her.'

She swallowed hard. 'Thank you for that,' she breathed shakily.

'So if you didn't do it deliberately she must have misunderstood something you wrote.'

Brenna gasped at the suggestion. 'I've never written anything that could be misunderstood in that way!' So much for his unexpected display of trust in her!

'Lesli *was* very emotional during her pregnancy,' he insisted. 'Maybe she took something you wrote about the two of us and turned it around on Grant and herself?' he probed.

'Nathan, I never used to write to Lesli about you,' she protested.

'Then what the hell could it have been?' he frowned his chagrin.

'Does Grant still have the letter?'

He shook his head. 'It's in the bedroom with Lesli, and he doesn't want to disturb her.'

'Then I'll get her to show it to me later.' She nodded, sure that once she had seen the letter she could explain away this misunderstanding. Although it wouldn't erase the admission she had made to Grant.

'Which only leaves the matter of us to discuss,' Nathan said quietly.

'Us?' she echoed faintly.

'This afternoon you agreed to marry me——'

'You can't still want to go through with that?' she gasped, knowing by the directness of his gaze that he was perfectly serious.

'After all,' he grated, 'you *do* own a quarter share in this ranch!'

'Nathan——'

He looked at her coldly. 'You're going to marry me,' he stated flatly. 'This time you'll go through with it and become my wife.'

'No,' Brenna shook her head frantically at the cold remoteness of him. 'No, Nathan!'

'What's so different from when you accepted my proposal this afternoon?' he grated dismissively. 'You've always believed I only wanted you to keep control of the ranch in the family, now you'll know that it's true!'

'I no longer believe that——'

'Really?' he scorned. 'You believed it last year when you ran out on me. Didn't you?'

'Nathan——'

'*Didn't you?*'

She flinched at the fury in his voice. 'Yes,' she admitted in a pained voice.

'And you believed it the night Christiana was born and we made love. Didn't you?'

'Yes,' her voice broke as she made the admission.

'And you believed it today when we made love.

Didn't you? Nathan prompted again.

'Yes. But——'

'And you believed it when you told me you loved me and that you would marry me. Didn't you?' His eyes were glacial.

'Nathan——'

'*Didn't you?*' he ground out with a fierceness that made her tremble.

'Yes,' she cried. 'Yes, yes, *yes*!' She was crying as she choked out the last.

Nathan was unmoved by her distress. 'Then it isn't going to bother you that you know it on our wedding day too!' he ground out remorselessly.

'Nathan, I told you, I no longer believe that,' she looked at him pleadingly.

'And just what's happened since then to change your mind?' he demanded.

'I knew I was wrong as soon as I saw your reaction to what Grant was saying. You——'

'I loved you,' he finished contemptuously. 'But do you know what I've learnt today, Brenna? I've learnt that love can die as quickly as it was born,' he told her coldly. 'That it can turn to contempt and loathing even more quickly.'

'Nathan, no,' she was crying brokenly now. 'I was wrong, I know I was wrong . . .'

'Past tense, Brenna,' he bit out scornfully. 'You'll be my wife, but in name only. I want your quarter of the ranch, but that's all I want from you. And if you even *attempt* to leave me again,' he warned as he read the panic in her eyes, 'I'll make love to you until you're too weak to do more than stand in front of the preacher and say

"I will"! You'll marry me this time, Brenna, make no mistake about it,' he promised grimly before forcefully leaving the room.

Hurt didn't even begin to describe what Nathan was feeling now, what was motivating him to act the way he was. He had loved her, had always loved her, and she had thrown that love back in his face.

She hadn't needed his cold anger just now to know she had lost his love irrevocably, she had seen that earlier as he listened to Grant. God, what a fool she had been! And how much she had lost because she hadn't trusted in the love they had always had for each other.

'You won't, will you?' Lesli stated sadly as she came into the room. 'You couldn't marry Nathan as things stand between you now.'

'Oh, Lesli, I——'

'It's all right.' Her sister held her tightly in her arms. 'Damn Grant and his temper,' she scowled as she held Brenna while she cried. 'I told him you couldn't be responsible.'

'I might not have ever written it, but I've always thought it,' Brenna admitted gruffly, wiping the tears from her cheeks. 'Grant suddenly asked you to marry him, and then when Patrick died we learnt that he'd left the ranch to all four of us, and . . .'

'Brenna, I saw Patrick's will today,' Lesli told her softly. 'I didn't need to see that it was dated only the week before Grant and I were married to know that I'd made a mistake in even half believing that letter.'

'So Grant——'

'Couldn't have known anything about his father's will when he asked me to marry him,' Lesli finished gently.

'I'm so glad,' said Brenna fervently.

'Not that it would have made any difference if the will had been dated the day he *asked* me to marry him,' Lesli admitted drily. 'I love Grant, and I've lived with him long enough to know that he loves me too. If I hadn't been pregnant, feeling as big as a house, and very insecure about the way I looked when that letter arrived I would never have taken any notice of it,' she sighed at her own gullibility.

'But I don't understand what I could have written to even make you think such a thing,' Brenna frowned.

'You didn't write anything,' Lesli shook her head unhesitatingly.

'But Grant said——'

'Grant was very angry when he found out what made me leave him,' Lesli explained with regret. 'He wasn't thinking straight. If he had been he would have known you would never have written to me anonymously like that——'

'Anonymously?' Brenna echoed sharply. 'You mean it wasn't something in one of my regular letters that influenced you to leave Grant?'

'He didn't tell you that the letter was typed and unsigned?' her sister frowned.

'No,' Brenna shook her head slowly, thoughts crowding her head. 'Can I see the letter?' she prompted softly.

'Of course,' Lesli nodded with a frown. 'I'll go and get it.'

Brenna both needed and dreaded seeing that letter. The fact that it hadn't been signed exonerated her completely, but that fact also made her fear what she was about to learn.

'Here you are,' Lesli returned, handing the single sheet of paper to Brenna.

As she quickly scanned its contents she felt a sinking feeling in her stomach. The words written there seemed so familiar, so *sickeningly* familiar!

'Where's the envelope it came in?' she asked abruptly, her hand tightly gripping the letter.

Lesli shrugged. 'I threw it away.'

'But the postmark,' Brenna protested. 'It could have helped you trace the person responsible.'

Lesli shrugged. 'I don't think so, London is a big place.'

London. It was all she needed to know. The person who had sent this letter was someone she had *trusted*.

CHAPTER TEN

'You do realise that Nathan is likely to string me up by the thumbs when he finds out I helped you get away from him like this?' Grant grimaced as he stood in the airport with Brenna waiting for her plane to leave. 'I'm supposed to be checking the hotel next door, not putting you on a plane that will take you away from him!'

'Then we'd better stay out of sight, hadn't we?' They stood in the area near her boarding gate, waiting for her flight to be called.

Grant looked at her anxiously. 'Are you sure you're doing the right thing? Nathan isn't going to take this lying down a second time, you know. He'll come after you.'

'I don't intend staying long in London,' she assured him softly. 'I'll be back.'

Grant sighed. 'If he doesn't find you first. The only reason he doesn't realise you're here now is that he's expecting you to get the London flight tomorrow as you originally planned to do.'

Because she still had a seat booked on that flight. But she had also managed to get a seat on a flight to Toronto tonight, and would pick up her connecting flight to England from there. As she had expected when she left the ranch tonight, Nathan was looking for her at all the Calgary hotels and motels.

In the meantime Grant had driven her to the airport, although he wasn't too happy about deceiving his brother in this way.

'I have to go to London,' she said determinedly.

'Look, I know I was angry earlier, but I've apologised, and I didn't really mean it about you leaving.'

'Grant, I'm not going because of that,' she assured him firmly. 'I want you to know your apology meant a great deal to me.'

'Yes. Well,' he looked sheepish. 'I should never have said those things to you. I'm sorry it's messed things up again between you and Nathan.'

'I don't think they'll ever be right between us,' she sighed.

'He's angry right now,' Grant conceded. 'But once he calms down he's going to love you the way that he always has. Hell, if he'd married you when he wanted to you would have beaten Lesli and me! But Dad persuaded him to let you go to college first before telling you how he felt about you.'

'I didn't know anything about that,' she gasped, her eyes wide.

'You would never have agreed to go to college if you had,' Grant said sarcastically. 'You were in love with Nathan even then, you would have married him if he had asked you.'

And if she had she would have spared herself all the pain of the last four years of denying her love for him. Time and distance had erected barriers between them that couldn't be broken down.

'Dad and Anna thought you should go to college first,' Grant added.

'Mum knew too?' she frowned.

His mouth twisted. 'I'm afraid my loving Lesli and Nathan loving you were foregone conclusions the moment we met. Oh, Nathan and I had to accept that you both had a lot of growing up to do first, but it was always the Jordan sisters for us,' he admitted. 'I couldn't be as patient as Nathan and let Lesli go off to become a lawyer before we were married! We thought it was all going to work out according to plan last Easter when you and Nathan became so close. Nathan withdrew into himself when you didn't come back,' he shook his head at the memory. 'None of us understood what had gone wrong, but Nathan said you'd made your decision and he wouldn't come after you. Lesli said you refused to even talk about Nathan in your letters.'

Because her mind had been poisoned, systematically, and very effectively.

But she couldn't tell Grant that, she needed time to take it in herself. And she had a couple of flights before her when she could do exactly that. Tomorrow she would face her enemy knowing who it was.

'That's all in the past now, Grant,' Brenna dismissed briskly.

He shook his head. 'Nathan is determined to find you this time.'

'So that he can marry me,' she nodded. 'I'll

come back to the ranch, but I don't think either of us are so self-destructive that we would marry each other!'

'I accept that there are misunderstandings between the two of you, but—Damn,' muttered Grant as her flight was called. 'You'll come back, Brenna?' he urged.

She nodded. 'But Nathan will never forgive me,' she sighed. 'And I certainly can't say I blame him.'

'Call us when you get home,' Grant hugged her tightly. 'Promise?'

She nodded slowly. 'I'll do that.'

He shrugged, knowing it was all he could expect for now, lifting his hand in final parting as she glanced back once before going through to get her flight.

The flight to Toronto seemed longer than it should have, the wait in the lounge while she waited for her connecting flight was even more so, and she was pale and hollow-eyed by the time she finally boarded the plane for London.

She took only a few minutes in her flat to shower and change, quickly checking her mail, dismissing most of it as unimportant, smiling as she read the brief card Carolyn had sent her from her weekend in New York, relieved when she read the letter from their publisher saying that story and drawings were great.

She gave her appearance only a cursory look before leaving, knowing she had matured considerably over the last twenty-four hours, that she had been disillusioned and hurt by one of the people she had loved.

He was sitting at his usual table, a paper propped up in front of him as he ate, a glass of water at his elbow, but she felt none of the warmth that usually engulfed her at seeing him again.

He wasn't aware of her presence as she walked across the room to him, and for a moment, as she looked into his handsome face, she wondered if she hadn't misjudged him. But then she knew that she hadn't, blinking back the tears as she straightened challengingly.

'Hello, Father.'

His hazel eyes registered his surprise before his face creased into a pleased smile. 'Hello, love,' he greeted her warmly. 'This is a lovely surprise!'

'Is it?' she said bitterly, wondering if she had ever really known this man, or if it had only been that side of himself that he had wanted her to see. She thought it was the latter.

'Of course, darling.' Andrew Jordan stood up to hold back a chair for her, and Brenna dropped down into it woodenly. 'All sorted out with Lesli now?' he asked lightly.

Brenna looked at him with cold green eyes. He looked the same to her as he always had, a recklessly handsome man, the drink giving him lines of dissipation beside his eyes that he shouldn't really have had at only forty-eight. Yes, he still looked the same, and yet she knew she would never feel the same about him again.

'Are you going to be too disappointed if I say yes?' she challenged, her eyes hard.

His eyes narrowed slightly, and it was the only

change in his expression. 'Don't you have that
the wrong way around, darling? I——'

'Don't call me that,' she snapped. 'And no, I'm
sure I don't have it at all wrong. Just tell me why
you did it,' she grated.

'Why did I do what?' he prevaricated in a
puzzled voice.

Why had he deliberately set out to alienate her
from the Wade family when they were reunited
four years ago? Why had he made her mistrust
Nathan's love for her by telling her Nathan had
to want her because of her share of the ranch,
that a Wade always had a reason for everything
he did? Why had he written that letter to Lesli
trying to shatter the very foundation of her
marriage? He certainly couldn't have been
motivated by love, of that she was certain.

She looked at him with dislike. 'I must have
been so easy to influence,' she said disgustedly. 'I
was already slightly in awe of the love I had for
Nathan when I came to England four years ago.
I'd felt a different sort of awe for Patrick since
the moment I met him, I was overwhelmed by
the way he always went determinedly after what
he wanted——'

'The way he went after your mother,' her
father accused harshly. 'We had a good marriage——'

'You had a lousy marriage,' she retorted. 'Even
I remember that you were rarely at home!'

'Because I was forced out by Patrick Wade,' he
defended. 'You know that was why I began to
drink, to stay away from home.'

Brenna looked at him with narrowed eyes. 'I know that *you* told me they had had an affair for years, but that nothing could come of it because of Patrick's marriage to Christine, her ill health meaning he couldn't divorce her,' she accused.

'Brenna, what's making you act like this?'

'I saw the letter you sent Lesli,' she snarled. '"A Wade takes what he wants even if he has to use someone else to do it",' she quoted vehemently. '"Grant only married you to keep control of the ranch, without your share of it you would have been thrown out of his life",' she quoted again. 'It was all too familiar, Father,' she said scornfully. 'It was almost word for word what you've been telling me over the years!'

'I didn't expect the stupid little fool to keep the letter,' he rasped disgustedly.

'You thought she would read it and then destroy it in her distress,' Brenna guessed cynically. 'But that the things you'd written would slowly eat away at her love for Grant until it was destroyed, the way my love for Nathan was so slowly eroded! But she didn't destroy the letter, she kept it, and as soon as I read it I knew who was responsible for writing it!'

'Okay,' he challenged. 'So I wrote my daughter a letter. There's nothing wrong in trying to protect her!'

Oh, she had been taken in so easily by this man during the last four years, had believed him when he said Patrick was the reason he began drinking, had claimed that he had become an outcast in his own marriage after Patrick and her mother met and fell in love, that after her mother had divorced him he had tried to keep the two girls, but that Patrick Wade had claimed in court that he was a drunk and not responsible enough to be a father to his own children, that Patrick had paid money into a bank account for him knowing he would drink himself into the grave with it.

But after seeing what her father had tried to do to Lesli she could see how he had distorted things, that her mother had probably turned to Patrick *because* of her husband's drinking, that her father had probably demanded that money as a pay-off for not pursuing his case to get custody of the girls. She had a feeling that this was a more accurate explanation of what had happened, and she felt ill at the way she had misjudged her mother and all the Wade men.

She gave a weary sigh. 'What really happened all those years ago?' she demanded.

'I told you——'

'This time I want the truth!' Her eyes shot flames at him.

'I'd be interested in hearing your account of that too!'

Brenna gasped at the sound of that coldly angry voice, turning to find Nathan seated at the table behind them. How long had he been sitting there? What was he *doing* here? *How* had he got here?

'What the hell . . .?' her father scowled at him as he stood up to occupy the seat between the two of them, his eyes narrowing as he fully took in the appearance of the younger man. 'A Wade!' he ground out with dislike.

Nathan nodded abruptly. 'A dreaded Wade,' he confirmed harshly, turning his attention to Brenna, clasping her hand as it moved restlessly on the table-top. 'It's going to be all right,' he told her gently. 'I understand now.'

Her avid gaze searched the harshness of his face. He had come after her, as Grant had said he would, but was it still in anger or in love? She couldn't tell just from looking at him.

He squeezed her hand tightly, maintaining that contact as he turned coldly compelling eyes on the older man. 'You were about to tell us what happened all those years ago . . .?' he prompted contemptuously. 'Your version of it, that is.'

Andrew Jordan flushed angrily. 'This is none of your business, boy——'

'The fact that it's my family you're maligning makes it my business, Jordan,' Nathan bit out. 'That Brenna is going to be my wife makes it doubly so,' he added challengingly.

Her father rose to that challenge. 'She isn't going to marry a Wade,' he snarled. 'She——'

'Brenna?' Nathan promptly softly.

She couldn't defy the command that told her to meet his gaze, almost burning at the fierceness of the love that shone there for her. Her fingers tightened convulsively about his; Grant *had* been right about this too; once Nathan had calmed down he had still loved her!

She turned to her father with glowing eyes. 'I'm going to *beg* to marry this Wade,' she told him fervently.

'You . . .!' Her father looked ready to explode. 'He's a *Wade*, Brenna,' he spluttered.

'I know,' she nodded happily.

'My God, you——'

'And needless to say you will not be invited to the wedding,' Nathan put in coldly.

'Hell would have to freeze over before I——'

'I *said* you weren't invited!' Nathan rasped. 'And neither of us is going to beg, Brenna,' he added softly. 'We're just going to get married as we would have done long ago without your father's poisonous lies coming between us.'

'Lies!' her father repeated explosively. 'Your father——'

'Never looked at another woman until long after my mother was dead,' Nathan ground out, his body tense beneath the grey jacket and black trousers, his white shirt unbuttoned at the throat. 'So that knocks down that theory for you becoming a drunk!'

'He and Anna——'

'Didn't meet until my mother had been dead for two years and she was divorced from you! Although I believe you tell a different version.' Nathan's eyes narrowed as Brenna gasped. 'Sweetheart?'

She swallowed hard. 'He said—he said . . .'

'Take your time,' he said gently. 'We have all day.' The last was added as a threat to her father.

'He told me that Patrick and my mother fell in love when I was still a baby, but that your father wouldn't leave your mother, and so for respectability's sake my mother stayed with him.

He said it was the reason he began to drink,' she revealed huskily.

'Ah, love,' Nathan sympathised huskily. 'What a bastard you are!' he turned on her father. 'She was only a kid, easily mixed up. But that was what you counted on, wasn't it?' he accused with dislike. 'When Anna divorced you Brenna was too young to realise what you were like, the drinking, the fits of temper, the violence——'

'Shut up!' her father ground out fiercely. 'Anna was unfaithful——'

'She never looked at another man during your marriage,' Nathan told him hardly. 'It was your guilt over your drinking that made you accuse her of affairs you knew didn't exist. You were a violent and abusive husband and father——'

'I never laid a hand on Brenna,' Andrew denied heatedly. 'Tell him, Brenna.'

She was too numbed by what she was hearing to tell Nathan anything! She had always remembered the father from her childhood as happy-go-lucky, a little irresponsible perhaps but basically a man who loved them all. She was hearing about a new, ugly side to his nature that she had only yesterday begun to guess at.

'Lesli has other memories,' Nathan rasped. 'And Brenna would eventually have realised what you were like too.' He looked at Brenna with gentle eyes. 'Why do you think Lesli would never have anything to do with him after you all left England?'

'I never thought about it. He always seemed so full of charm, so—I didn't know,' she shook her head dazedly.

'I'm sure he made sure you never found out once you came here to college,' Nathan acknowledged grimly. 'I put the distance that was widening between you and the family down to the fact that you were growing away from us, making a life for yourself here. I had no idea you were seeing your father again until I came here last month.' His mouth tightened. 'I suppose I should have realised then that he was behind all this, but you said he had changed, and I wanted to believe that was true. For your sake.'

She shook her head. 'You were right, he's sick. He——'

'You're letting yourself be fooled by him just as your mother was by his father,' her father scorned. 'They took my daughters away from me, paid me off with money I never asked for——'

'Anna didn't want you near Lesli and Brenna once she left here,' Nathan bit out. 'And the money my father gave you was supposed to pay for you to go to a clinic to dry out and then support you until you found a job.' His mouth twisted scornfully. 'But I'm sure you put it to a different use!'

Andrew flushed. 'Whichever way you look at it your father tried to buy me off——'

'You were given money to try and make something of your life,' Nathan corrected harshly. 'And my father only did that for Anna's sake. Personally he couldn't give a damn if you'd returned to the sewer you'd crawled from! And neither can I.'

'You damned——'

'This may be a public restaurant,' Nathan ground out with chilling intensity, 'but if you call me a bastard I'm going to put you on the floor where you belong!'

Her father paled. 'The Wades and their damned power! You all deserve each other,' he said bitterly. 'Lesli and Grant. You and Brenna,' his mouth turned back contemptuously.

'I don't understand why you wanted to hurt Lesli and me,' Brenna looked at him with pained eyes. 'What did we ever do to you?'

'Nothing,' he rasped. 'But Anna and Patrick were dead, and the two of you were very much alive!'

She swallowed hard at his vehemence. 'And what you told me last summer about dying?'

'Aren't we all?' he gave a harsh laugh as she flinched. 'I could see that you were weakening towards Wade's son, that something had happened between you during that Easter break, and I knew that once a Wade declares his love he claims what's his.'

'So you invented the visit to your doctor and the fact that he said you only had a couple of years left to live!' she choked, remembering how she had felt after her father had told her the alcoholism Patrick had driven him to by stealing his wife from him caused his health to deteriorate so badly that it was slowly killing him. She had known then that she couldn't return to Nathan that summer, that she couldn't live with him knowing his father was responsible for her father's death. And it had all been a lie.

'Yes,' Andrew confirmed with satisfaction.

'You disgust me,' Nathan told him with dislike. 'Brenna and Lesli are your daughters!'

'You know...' Andrew's mouth twisted, 'I once toyed with the idea of letting Brenna think Patrick could be her father,' he smiled with relish. 'Now wouldn't that have been interesting?' he mocked softly.

A nerve pulsed in Nathan's tightly clenched jaw. 'You *are* sick,' he said with vehemence. 'But you won't have the opportunity to lie to Brenna any more,' he bit out grimly. 'If you ever come near her again you'll regret it!'

Andrew sighed. 'There's no point now she knows the truth,' he dismissed. 'Pity, it was fun while it lasted,' he drawled.

Brenna couldn't believe that this was her father speaking, the man who had convinced her he had been so badly treated by the Wade family that for a while she had been sure she didn't like them either. This man cared nothing for anyone, probably never had; he only wanted to hurt and destroy, and had used her vulnerability as a way of doing that. God, she had even been the one to confide her confusion to him over Patrick's will, had given him another weapon to use to his advantage. He had used her to hurt all the people she loved.

'Come on, Brenna,' Nathan stood up, his hand grasping her arm now. 'We're leaving.'

She had taken a couple of steps with him before she stopped, and pulled out of his grasp, moving to stand next to her father as she drew

back her hand and hit him with all the pain and
hate inside her. 'I don't suppose you're interested,' she ground out, 'but you have a
granddaughter. Her name is Christiana Wade.
And in about another eight months you're going
to have another grandchild—and he or she will be
a Wade too! But you'll never see either of them,'
she assured him before turning away and leaving
the restaurant with Nathan, oblivious of the
shocked faces of the other diners after she had
struck her father.

Dry sobs racked her body as she lay against
Nathan's chest in the taxi, his arms possessively
about her.

'That wasn't exactly the way I envisaged being
told I'm going to be a father,' he murmured
indulgently. 'But as far as dramatics go it was . . .
It *was* true, wasn't it?' he asked anxiously.

'I'm as sure as I can be without having a test,'
Brenna nodded, clinging to him.

'Well, if you aren't now, we can always make
sure that you are,' he announced arrogantly.

'How can you still love me after this?' She
looked up at him uncertainly.

'I've always loved you. I always will.'

She frowned. 'That day you came to Cumbria,
you said you didn't.'

Nathan shook his head. 'I said I no longer
"imagined" I loved you; I've never imagined it,
I've always *known* it!'

'But how can you ever forgive me?' she choked.
'I believed all those lies my father told me,' she
groaned at her stupidity.

'The thing is everything he told you sounded so damned plausible,' Nathan told her gently, smoothing back the wisps of hair at her temples that had escaped the confining combs. 'And I'm not completely without blame in all this; I should have realised what was going on.'

'How could you——'

'Brenna, I've loved you ever since I can remember,' he cut in huskily. 'I should have looked more deeply into the changes in you.'

'He told me that he'd been bought off,' she shivered. 'That Mummy had been dazzled by Patrick's wealth, that Grant had paid the price of his freedom to keep control of the ranch in the family——'

'And that I was doing the same thing with you, hence your remarks about the Wades always paying for what they want,' Nathan finished grimly. 'Only that wasn't the way Dad looked at it at all. Grant and Lesli's wedding was already arranged, and he knew it was only a matter of time before I proposed to you, and loving you both as he did he wanted you and Lesli to have some independence of your own. Darling, something you and your father seem to have overlooked in all this is that Lesli still owns her quarter of the ranch, and even if we get married——'

'When,' she corrected sharply.

'When we get married,' he drawled in satisfaction. 'Your quarter of the ranch will still be your own; a wife's property doesn't automatically become her husband's any more!'

'I've been so stupid,' she groaned.

'Not stupid,' he chided. 'Just misguided. Anyway,' he added briskly, 'Grant and I think we've come up with a solution to the ranch problem, if you and Lesli are agreeable.'

She looked at him frowningly, not liking the sound of this at all. 'Oh?'

He nodded. 'We're going to sell it.'

'*What?*' she gasped disbelievingly, staring at him as if he had gone mad. As she felt sure he must have done!

He shrugged. 'We had a talk yesterday before you did your disappearing act, and decided that it was the only thing to do to convince you and Lesli that it's you we want and not the ranch——'

'No,' she told him determinedly. 'That ranch belongs to the family; it always has!'

'But you hate it——'

'Not enough to ask you to give it up!' she protested. 'I'm sure Lesli will feel the same way.'

'She does,' he nodded. 'But as you know we only need a majority to sell and we thought you——'

'No,' she said again.

'What about all those "lovely little calves that are ultimately fattened up for slaughter"?' he reminded her drily.

'Hm.' A frown marred her brow.

'I did come up with another solution on the flight over here,' he told her softly.

Pain darkened her eyes. 'Please don't say it's that we don't get married!'

'Oh, you're marrying me, Brenna Jordan,' he

assured her fiercely, his arms tightening about her. 'As soon as we get back. Which reminds me, you promised you wouldn't run out on me again——'

'I was coming back,' she cut in quickly. 'I just had to—had to see my father. But how did you get here so quickly?' she frowned.

'By getting on the same plane you did and following you,' he revealed grimly. 'Lesli finally relented and told me what you were doing, and I managed to get on your flight by the skin of my teeth! When Lesli told me you intended coming back I had a feeling you knew something about that letter you weren't telling any of us, and so I followed you to the restaurant too.'

'I'm so glad you did!' Brenna pressed herself against him.

'Do you want to hear the alternative solution or would you rather we just made love on the back seat of this taxi?' he drawled.

She looked about them dazedly. 'I would rather we went up to my flat and made love,' she told him huskily as the taxi came to a halt outside her home.

'That's what I'd like to do too,' Nathan said gruffly, paying the driver before following her inside. 'Very slowly,' he murmured as he carried her through to her bedroom. 'We can talk about your father later.'

She shivered at the mention of him. 'Much later,' she agreed, pulling him down to her on the bed.

He looked down at her with eyes darkened by

passion. 'What about my alternative solution?' he teased her haste in undressing him.

'I don't care where we live as long as we're together,' she assured him as she pulled him fiercely into her.

'I'm sure he's too young to be sitting up there,' Brenna watched the two in the corral anxiously from her sitting position on the fence.

'Rubbish!' A proud grin split Nathan's lean features as he held his son on the stallion's back.

Nine months almost to the day after Christiana's birth Patrick Nathan Wade had made his entrance into the world with a loud wail of indignation. And as Nathan had held the tiny replica of himself in his arms only seconds after birth, Brenna had looked on with proud pleasure.

But she hadn't expected their son to be hoisted up on Samson's back when he was only nine months old and not even walking yet!

'Stop fussing.' Carolyn sat beside her on the fence, her designer jeans not daring to pick up even the slightest speck of dust, the thin gold wedding band glinting on her left hand. 'He's loving it!'

Patrick was chuckling so hard that couldn't be doubted, his black curls bouncing, his grey eyes filled with merriment, his little chubby hands clinging to the reins, his confidence in his father's ability to take care of him complete.

Brenna dismissed her anxiety to look about them with satisfaction. Nathan's 'alternative solution' had been to divide the ranch into two homesteads, Grant and Lesli continuing with the cattle while he and Brenna branched out into seriously breeding horses. It was something Nathan had always taken an interest in, and in his first year it had been obvious he was going to make a success of it. The proof of that was all about them. As an 'alternative solution' it had been ideal. Although at only nine months old Patrick was becoming as fond of steak as his father was!

'Ride him, cowboy!' Nick joined them at the side of the corral, encouraging Patrick.

Brenna gave him a scathing look. 'A fine example of a godfather you are!'

He grinned up at her. 'By the time he's two years old he'll be riding as well as his old man!'

'Wait until you get one of your own,' she warned. 'Then we'll see who worries!'

Nick laid a familiar hand on his wife's thigh. 'We're still practising,' he murmured with satisfaction.

Carolyn laughed happily. 'I think we're about to go in for some serious training!'

Nathan laughed at Nick's stunned expression at this news as he walked over to join them, Patrick sitting trustingly in his arms. 'Here,' he handed Patrick to the other man. 'He needs his diaper changing, you'd better learn to do it before yours gets here!'

'But I . . . But—Carolyn!' Nick looked at her disbelievingly.

She jumped down off the fence. 'Don't look so stunned, darling,' she mocked. 'We've been having the most marvellous time trying the last three months!'

'Yes, but—you could have chosen somewhere a little less public to tell me,' he complained as the two to them walked with Patrick towards the wood-construction ranch house. 'You would have looked pretty stupid if I'd fainted or something.'

'That's during the birth, silly.' She took Patrick from him.

'I feel ill now,' he told her irritably. 'Carolyn, you should have . . .'

Nathan chuckled as the other couple disappeared into the house, his arm about Brenna's shoulders. 'She'll be surprising him the rest of his life!'

'Yes,' Brenna smiled, looking up at the husband she adored.

Nathan's eyes darkened as he met the flame of desire in hers. 'I think it's time I showed the mother of my son that I'm perfectly capable of taking care of him—and her,' he murmured huskily.

'We have guests arriving for dinner in half an hour,' she reminded him as he swung her up in his arms, striding towards the house with determined steps.

'Only Grant and Lesli, and they're used to coming for dinner and having to eat on their own!'

They grinned at each other as they shared the memory of the night Lesli and Grant had come to dinner on the very night Brenna had been declared fit after Patrick's birth. The other couple had been greeted by the housekeeper, had eaten dinner, admired Patrick, all without Brenna and Nathan having put in an appearance, lost in the wonder of being physically close again. They hadn't even realised until days later what they had done! It was now a standing family joke that you took your chances when you dined with Brenna and Nathan.

'Besides, we're practising ourselves, aren't we?' he reminded her throatily.

They had decided that it was time for Patrick to have a little brother or sister. Brenna had had an easy pregnancy and childbirth with him and both of them wanted another two or three children.

She shook her head. 'We're already perfect,' she welcomed him down on to her body as they lay on the bed, knowing that they had put the past behind them now, that they loved each other enough to surmount any obstacle.

Together.

Coming Next Month

927 AN ELUSIVE MISTRESS Lindsay Armstrong
An interior designer from Brisbane finally finds a man to share the rest of her life with—only to have her ex-husband return and reawaken feelings she'd thought were hidden forever.

928 ABODE OF PRINCES Jayne Bauling
In mysterious Rajasthan, Fate prompts a young woman to redefine her understanding of love and friendship. But the man she meets and loves will hear nothing of her breaking her engagement for him.

929 POPPY GIRL Jaqueline Gilbert
Dreams of wealth don't overwhelm a prospective heiress. But a certain Frenchman does. If only she didn't come to suspect his motives for sweeping her off her feet.

930 LOVE IS A DISTANT SHORE Claire Harrison
A reporter with a knack for getting to the heart of the matter disturbs the concentration of a young woman planning to swim Lake Ontario. Surely she should concentrate on one goal at a time.

931 CAPABLE OF FEELING Penny Jordan
In sharing a roof to help care for her boss's niece and nephew, a young woman comes to terms with her inability to express love. Is it too late to change the confines of their marriage agreement?

932 VILLA IN THE SUN Marjorie Lewty
Villa Favorita is the private paradise she shared with her husband—until his fortunes plummeted and he drove her away. Now she has been asked to handle the sale. Little does he know how closely her husband follows the market.

933 LAND OF THUNDER Annabel Murray
The past is a blank to this accident victim. She feels a stranger to her "husband." Worse, their new employer touches something disturbing within her. Something's terribly wrong here.

934 THE FINAL PRICE Patricia Wilson
In Illyaros, where her Greek grandfather lies ill, her ex-husband denies both their divorce and her right to remarry. Yet he was unfaithful to her! No wonder she hasn't told him about the birth of their son.

Available in November wherever paperback books are sold, or through Harlequin Reader Service:

In the U.S.
P.O. Box 1397
Buffalo, N.Y.
14240-1397

In Canada
P.O. Box 2800, Postal Station A
5170 Yonge Street
Willowdale, Ontario M2N 6J3

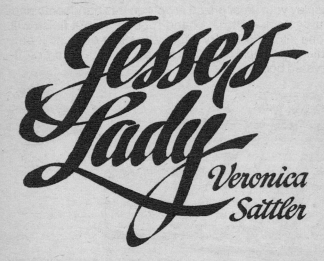

Take 4 novels and a surprise gift FREE

HARLEQUIN HISTORICAL

Explore love with Harlequin in the Middle Ages, the Renaissance, in the Regency, the Victorian and other eras.

Relive within these books the endless ages of romance, set against authentic historical backgrounds. Two new historical love stories published each month.

HIST-A-1